A Kind of Wild Justice

BERNARD ASHLEY

A Kind of Wild Justice

Illustration by Charles Keeping

OXFORD UNIVERSITY PRESS
OXFORD   NEW YORK   MELBOURNE

F

Oxford University Press, Walton Street, Oxford OX2 6DP

OXFORD   LONDON   GLASGOW
NEW YORK   TORONTO   MELBOURNE   AUCKLAND
KUALA LUMPUR   SINGAPORE   HONG KONG   TOKYO
DELHI   BOMBAY   CALCUTTA   MADRAS   KARACHI
NAIROBI   DAR ES SALAAM   CAPE TOWN

and associated companies in
BEIRUT   BERLIN   IBADAN   MEXICO CITY   NICOSIA

Oxford is a trade mark of Oxford University Press

First published 1978
Reprinted 1984

British Library Cataloguing in Publication Data
Ashley, Bernard
A kind of wild justice.
I. Title
823'.9'1J   PZ7.A8262   78–40281

ISBN 0–19–271417–1

5006
|

Printed in Hong Kong

For my family, and especially for
Alfred and Harold

I should like to thank Edwin Holbrook,
George Hore and G. Riat Singh for their
helpful advice on various matters of
custom and the law.

The extract from 'Last Snow' by Andrew Young
is taken from Andrew Young's 'Complete Poems'
and is used by permission of
Martin Secker & Warburg Limited.

'Revenge is a kind of wild justice;
which the more man's nature runs to,
the more ought law to weed it out.'

Francis Bacon—Essay 4 'Of Revenge'.

I

The strength in Charlie Whitelaw's straight back physically dominated the front of the coach just as the strength of his will ruled the children he drove. The lattice of stitched scars may have been hidden beneath his white shirt, but there wasn't a boy who hadn't heard about them and wondered at the evidence of three surgeons' patient skills and the guts of the man who had borne it. And not one of them fiddled with the air vents or tipped out ashtrays in Charlie's coach. The teachers swivelled their heads and shouted to show off a bit of order-keeping; and it was all for Charlie's benefit, because they wouldn't have done it for the head.

The swimming coach stopped outside the school with a final judder and Charlie, after a glance in the interior mirror, got up from his seat and turned round. The talking stopped; no one moved; Mr. Fleming tensed himself, ready.

'Right,' said Charlie, 'don't leave nothing behind,' and he nodded at the teacher, the signal to move the children off. Then the big man sat and tapped his fingers on the steering wheel while he watched the children file off in the near-side glass.

The last boy to jump down the steep steps was the smallest: wet-headed and white-clean from the baths, his grey towel hanging from beneath his elbow like a dead rabbit, he walked into the school apart, keeping behind the other swimmers, and yet moving just fast enough not to be caught up by Mr. Fleming. He knew about Charlie's scars, all about them, the same as the rest of the kids; but seeing the man every week reminded Ronnie Webster about things, and even if he'd been a brilliant swimmer he wouldn't have felt any better about Mondays. There were some sorts of things you forgot, and there were some sorts of things you remembered. Like, you might forget the sounds of letters in reading, but you never forgot it when someone said they'd do to your back what they'd done to Charlie Whitelaw's.

Without raising his eyes from the floor Ronnie Webster snuffled his way up and through the school until he came to the class-room door. A quick glance up from under his frown told him that she was sitting there waiting; but he rarely altered his speed to please teachers.

'Get a move on, Webster,' Miss Neame said sharply, 'I can't wait all day, even if the B.B.C. were to let me. And don't drip that wet all over my pamphlets....'

Bloody *Poetry Time*! Ronnie sat down at his solitary seat among the chalk dust under the blackboard. It had always been the same, right from the Infants: wet hands, sandy hands, dirty hands, always some teacher having a go about the damage he'd do to her precious books with his hands. Miss Lovejoy had been the first. 'Ronnie Webster, wash your hands before you dare touch *Squirrel Nutkin*!' And if she'd shouted it once she'd shouted it a million times. Not that he was ever anywhere near the rotten books. All he knew was that ever since he could remember he'd hardly ever seemed to be allowed to face in one direction for more than ten seconds at a time; he had spent his life being shuttled between his place and the teacher's, between his class-room and Mrs. Monks' office, and between the lower hall and the washing sinks in the lavatories.

But he wasn't bothered. He couldn't be. No kid who lived under the real threat of having his back broken by the Bradshaws could have much feeling left over to worry about Miss Lovejoy, or Mrs. Monks, or clean hands for looking at *Squirrel Nutkin*.

Just he and his dad had been at home at the time, when Bernie Bradshaw, the tall broad one with the cream suit and the brown bald head, had stood blocking the light out from

2

the living-room, one ringed hand resting on the tap like a fleshy spider; while his brother Roy, the hard case, had stood kicking the lobby door with his heel, chewing loudly. And with hinted smirks and serious eyes the warning had been given.

'One word outta place, Steve, my son, an' we break the kid's back, right?'

They'd both taken their eyes off his nodding father and stared at Ronnie, who could still remember trying to get behind the greasy cooker.

'No messin' about, no second chances or none o' that, right?'

And both Ronnie and his white-faced father had known they would keep their word. The only trouble was, while Ronnie never forgot, his father's memory could be drowned along with his sorrows—and brandy or best bitter always seemed to make his mouth go slack.

For four years now Ronnie had lived on the narrow ledge of real fear, sick some days with distrust of his father, with no end to his pain in sight, for there was no sign which could ever say he was out of danger; there couldn't be; not while the Bradshaws kept Shepherds Gate in their fat-fingered waistcoat pockets; nor while Steve Webster could still be drunk into nicking and driving a hot motor. So Ronnie had learned how to see everywhere at once without looking, how to read a face for safety, how to run in a zigzag, kick where it hurt, and knock off someone's dinner money when he thought he needed to stay out late and walk the long way home. But he had never learned how to care for a book; nor hardly even which way to hold it up.

Miss Neame sat over the transistor radio on her desk as if she were spiriting the voice up and out of it by stern concentration, although once it got out the man's Yorkshire warmth was soon cancelled out by her frosty face. But Ronnie, alone under the blackboard behind her, was unaffected by her face; and in any case, he could always feed from his

3

private store of secrets about her if she turned nasty. It was a useful trick he'd picked up, being aware that knowing private things about people kept them in their place in your mind. So when she came on strong about him kicking the chair legs or something, he'd think about her rubbing ointment into her swollen ankles under the desk, and that helped to keep her from riling him too much. Like the Bradshaws had discovered long ago, when you'd got something good on someone they ceased to be a threat any more.

He pushed the top of his mouth up under his nose in a moist pout and sniffed the chlorine on his skin, then he rubbed the length of his rolled towel up his face, and sighed. Load of crap, poetry, he thought—but at least you didn't have to write nothing while it was on. And she couldn't tell whether you were listening to the radio or thinking about things on your own. So he usually thought about things on his own. And today he needed to, even more than on most Mondays.

It was his dad again. It didn't take a genius to know he was being got at to do another job, and there wasn't much chance he'd turn it down, not only because Val wanted it—but because it was Bernie Bradshaw who was asking. Some pressures were too strong to fight against, even when you wanted to.

'Nothing to it, Steve,' Bernie had said. 'Saturdays no one thinks nothing's gonna happen except City East are gonna lose. And with all that crowd turning out round a quarter to five the law's gonna be well boxed-in....'

That much had been said in Ronnie's hearing while his dad had been watching an old film. Bernie didn't mind who heard because no one ever told, not even the nippers; and he knew Ronnie wouldn't; especially not Ronnie Webster.

'And what about the force of that last line, the picture the poet was painting? What about you, Webster? Did it have enough life for you?'

She'd turned round and was staring at him: a smarmy

4

voice, O.K., but the old ratbag knew she'd caught hi.

Ronnie shrugged. 'I dunno.' His shrug said he o
care, either.

'Well, I'll read it to you again, and *then* perhaps you'
know....'

So she was going to see him out, then. Silly fat cow.

> "". . . And one green spear,
>   Stabbing a dead leaf from below,
>   Kills winter at a blow.""

'Doesn't that paint a picture, Webster?'

What the hell *was* she going on about, 'paint a picture'?
He sniffed. 'Yeah.' His voice was resigned and bored. But
just saying something seemed to change her mind and shut
her up, somehow. Something did, anyway.

'Yes, I thought so, too....'

Miss Neame turned round to the rest of the class and
went on to them in her special poetry voice, floating on over
Ronnie's head. She'd definitely backed off, then. Had to
have a go, hadn't she, but enough was enough. Now, let off,
he went back to remembering Bernie Bradshaw, tricky as a
flick-knife, stabbing away at his dad with words.

'I'm dead certain who I want. It's cut and dried. It's all
set and there's nothing can go wrong, Stevie, son. It's definitely down to you for the driving....' He smiled. 'You
see, none of the lads won't hear of no one else. It's important, Stevie, or I wouldn't 'ave come round myself, would
I....?'

Bernie was sitting in an armchair as if all he'd come for
was to sell insurance; persuasive, yes, but as if a straight 'no'
would have merely sent him away disappointed. Only
Ronnie knew it wasn't like that. No way. He'd clear off all
right, but he'd soon send someone round to show just how
deep his disappointment went....

'Now, don't take too long making up your mind, my son.
But I don't wanna know tonight. Come down The Rose

my mind at rest, eh?' Bernie suddenly got
to standing up in one smooth economic
stration of strength, and Steve Webster
to stay staring at the jingling set.
e said. 'I might do that. Nice to know
yourself, i'n it? Still wanted, like....'
true. I've always thought so myself, Stevie. It's
always favourite to be wanted. Better than being found
wanting, eh?' And Bernie Bradshaw had gone, before Steve
could say any more.

'You great berk! Stupid bloody fool! You wanna get us
done, do you?' His wife's thin voice, unglamorous in its
anger like the small blazing eyes without their lashes, hit
Steve as the door slammed.

'Don't tell me,' Steve said, back staring at the television
again, 'you're cross about something.... Don't you reckon,
Ron?'

'Cross?' Val Webster shouted at him. 'Leave off! Cross
ain't in it! God you're so thick it ain't true! You're thick
when you're sober and thicker when you're drunk! Look, I
don't care about you, but stupid talk like that to *'im* could
get the rotten lot of us done!' Her small bloodless face
threatened to collide like a comet into his as she came at
him. 'You're *nothin'* now, *nobody*! The odd bit of driving
you do for other people don't keep us in fags. You're lucky
to get asked, an' you 'ave to go off like that! With *'im* of all
people!'

She turned her back on him as if she were more resigned
to his stupidity than angry with it. She dropped her voice.
'You won't never learn, you won't ... Ronnie, you seen my
cigarettes?'

'Eh?' Ronnie was just coming out of his scare at being in
the same room as Bernie Bradshaw, just beginning to fill
more of the armchair he was in. 'On the cooker....'

'Oh, yeah.' She scratched two yellow fingers through hair
which was straight and white to the fine roots. Then she

6

went once more at Steve. 'Listen, mate, you go down there tomorrow without fail and tell 'im you'll do it. Put 'im straight 'fore he thinks he needs to sort us out.' She stared hard at him before she finally stumped out of the room to get her cigarettes.

Steve yawned loudly and turned to look at Ronnie. 'Don't they make a bloody fuss?' he said. 'Women?'

Ronnie was frowning, a perpetual mark on his forehead above the lowered lids. He sniffed, and he scratched the tingling itch down his back against the chair.

'Pamphlets in!'

Mechanically, Ronnie held his out for Errol to collect. Yes, his dad'd say he'd do it tonight all right. The stupid idiot. But what else could he do? Val was right. There wasn't any saying no. Every now and then it happened. A quiet time would come to an end like this, and his father, instead of being easy with him, would suddenly get all jumpy as he got involved doing something for the Bradshaws. Then after, he'd get drunk for a fortnight, and while Val wore her new fur coat, Ronnie would be left to sit watching the telly, scared with every click of the door in case someone thought his dad had said too much. It was all right for them, Steve and Val. Perhaps they could forget one diabolical threat among so many—life was all threats, round here— but it was on *his* back; and he wasn't a great bull like Charlie Whitelaw; he was only a kid; and he was well scared.

Perhaps it was that living on a knife-edge that had isolated Ronnie. Miss Neame thought it was his inability to read which set him apart—there were few as bad as Webster in the school, she'd complained, until she'd got some extra help with him. But Mr. Fleming disagreed. A boy who kicked at a football as if he were scattering a seed dandelion, and who went in the shallow end of the baths with the confidence of an old lady at physiotherapy, could never hope to be one of the lads. But Ronnie knew differently. Life might be a load of games for the rest of them, playing out after school, having birthdays, watching telly, going to scouts on Fridays: but for him it was different. He didn't play cops and robbers, and talk about watching thrillers on the box: he was on the near edge of being part of the real thing; and a nasty accident, to him, could never be someone falling off the P.E. apparatus: it was the thought of a pick handle across the brittle of his back.

'Try it,' the teachers would say, 'try building up the words like the others do....' But there had never been any sense of purpose in that c...a...t crap, and there never would be.

And that was what set him apart.

Now, on that Monday of decision, Ronnie suddenly found himself faced about again and shunted off for more of Miss Lessor's extra reading help. There were just the two of them, Ronnie and the girl, Manjit Mirza, in a converted cloakroom with the young woman; two very different kettles of fish—for while Manjit's lack of English would soon be made good, Ronnie's lack of interest would never be.

Once more, as on most days, Ronnie sat there and made Miss Lessor force him to do something.

'Come on, Ronnie Webster,' she said, as breezy and determined as a prevailing wind, 'I'm going to get some work done with you if it kills us both, so make your mind up to it. . . .' And she gave him some cards to match, pictures with simple words to set against them.

Ronnie looked at them and shuffled them about, little glossy-covered drawings of a net, a nut, a can and a cot, and with his jaw cupped low over the table in his leaning hand, dead set against her, he sullenly put one word against each picture—and chance alone gave him one right out of four.

Manjit, at the end of the table, was trying harder, and judging by Miss Lessor's encouraging grunts she was doing well. Ronnie breathed his disgust out through his nostrils as her sense of success spiced the air, an incensed snort that raised Miss Lessor's head.

8

'Catch a cold swimming, did you, Ronnie?' she asked, not prepared to let even a sullen sigh go unremarked. 'Well, let's see how you've done....'

Ronnie watched her looking at his cards with the casual eye of a man on a bus giving up his ticket to the inspector. If there was anything wrong it wouldn't be his fault.

'Wrong, right, wrong, wrong.' Miss Lessor sighed herself, and then tried to look on the bright side. 'Good. You've got "net". Do you go fishing, Ronnie, with your dad?'

Ronnie silently shook his head, almost an imperceptible movement. No, he didn't go fishing with his dad. Neither of them was the patient, fishing, sort.

'Oh, well, never mind. But how can you say "can" begins with an "n"? Eh?'

Ronnie didn't know. He shrugged and turned his head away from Miss Lessor; but that faced him at Manjit, so with his mouth pressed into a long-suffering line he looked up at the ceiling.

'Look down here, please. "Ner" for "net", "ner" for "nut", "ker" for "can" and "ker" for "cot". See? It's just a question of knowing the sounds and building them up. Once you've mastered that you've got nothing to worry about. Yes?'

Miss Lessor looked at him, to see him nod to acknowledge how simple it would be. But he just shrugged again. She leaned closer, confidentially, and her long hair brushed the cards on the table, mixing them up again.

'I know you think I don't understand, Ronnie. But I do, you know. I *know* it isn't easy. But you've already won half the battle if you'll only let someone help you. If you want to learn to read, and you'll trust me, we've as good as done it. Now then....'

She had spoken very softly, her face so close to his that he could smell the perfume in her make-up. But he could see the black girl at the end of the table, and his toes curled in his boots.

9

Stupid bloody teachers!

'Take these,' Miss Lessor said, pressing the small yellow cards into the palm of his hand as if she were making him a present of a golden sovereign, 'and practise at odd moments; get your mum or your dad to have a go with you....'

He wrinkled his nose and he shrugged again. It looked non-committal, perhaps distrusting. But it was a lot more than that. It was the nearest he could get to saying, 'Get lost. Get off my back....'

'If you're 'ungry, Ronnie, get yourself some chips. . . .'

Ronnie sat in an armchair picking at the word cards in his pocket while an old cowboy film raced across the television screen. Val slapped twenty pence on the fire surround and bent to zip up her long white boots. 'An' switch it off 'fore you go to bed....'

Only Ronnie's eyes moved, just a brief flicker in her direction. He said nothing, but he'd taken it all in: her little eyes made up big, her long straight hair all shiny, her tightest sweater on, and her platform heels to make her stand sexy.

'Steve, 'urry up, for God's sake. Don't keep 'im 'anging about....' Val looked at herself in the mirror. Yes, she'd do, her straight face said; she'd go down all right. 'Come on! If you're late 'e might think you ain't coming....'

'Oh, 'elp: the end of the world!' Steve came in, spruced up himself, with his blond beard trimmed and a new black shirt on.

'Yeah, it just might be, mate!'

'Oh, do shut up!' He sounded as if he really didn't care: but he'd squirted under his arms, and he'd made sure he had a couple of tenners in his pocket to take care of a few drinks.

Without waiting, Val made for the door. Then she suddenly stopped. 'What's this?' she said, suspiciously, picking a small square of yellow card from the floor, frowning at finding something she shouldn't out of one of Steve's pockets. '"Net"? Oh, it's yours,' she said, immediately off-hand. '"R.W." This something from your school?' And she flicked it at Ronnie like an empty cigarette packet.

Ronnie scowled and stuffed it away quickly. Lessor's rotten word-cards! Baby stuff! A right show-up!

But Steve took no notice. He followed Val, still combing his hair, and neither of them said any more to Ronnie: so Ronnie said nothing more to them. But once he'd heard the bang of them going he moved his chair so that he could see both the television and the living-room door, and with the lights full on he gave the door and the picture equal parts of his attention: just in case his dad went and said the wrong thing to anyone tonight....

The Rose was crowded early, although to a casual visitor it would have been hard to tell why. There was nothing to be seen which made it stand out from a thousand other shiny bars with mirrored walls: there was no promise of a disco or go-go dancers to bring an early crowd, no darts match to be played or pile of pennies to be knocked over by a local boxer: and the beer was the same mass-produced liquid which filled a million metal barrels in cellars around London. But judging by the way everyone's head turned towards the door whenever it swung open, the crowd of noisy men and quiet, brightly dressed women were waiting for some-thing to happen, or for someone to come.

There was a second's break in the conversation, almost like pulling out the radio plug, when Steve and Val Webster walked in; but the anticipation wasn't for them; there were a few non-committal nods and, 'Oh, 'ello Stevie,' from one of the corners, but nothing more, and the pair of them were left to elbow-in at the besieged bar and drink alone. No one would want to know them just yet.

After the bustle of buying the drinks, when Steve's atten-tion had to be devoted to catching Big Terry the guv'nor's eye with his waving tenner, the two of them stood facing each other and suddenly found that they had nothing to say: the only thing they might have wanted to talk about was what had brought them there, and they daren't do that, so they stood and sipped, and looked all round, until their silence in all that noise seemed to be shouting itself to the whole bar—and at last Val dredged-up something, just to keep themselves looking normal.

'That ring,' she said, 'd'you reckon that diamond was real? In Lewis's window? That one two 'undred pounds. . . .'

'I dunno, do I?'

'If it was it must've been flawed. It wasn't 'alf big. . . .' She kept her face towards Steve, but her eyes were all round the bar, and her mind was somewhere else.

Steve was getting impatient now and slightly tense. And one drink wasn't going to do much about that. He put his hand in his back pocket again. But before he could get it out another silence suddenly stopped him, and he swung his head to the door; someone else was coming in; and somehow, now, in the way the door paused importantly before being fully opened, he knew that this was it; at last; what had kept him awake all night, worrying, was here. The Bradshaws had come.

Little Danny Diamond the flyweight boxer held the door open and in walked the Bradshaws as if they'd come to declare something open, smiling the impersonal smiles of the well-known, their eyes darting cautiously round the room.

People might easily have walked past them in the street. Neither of them was flamboyantly dressed. Bernie, broader and shorter, wore a quiet, dark, wool suit, looking back to winter; while Roy, taller and harder, like an off-duty footballer, anticipated summer in his fitted floral shirt. It was as if he felt the March cold no more than he ever felt anything.

Bernie murmured a few greetings as they walked across

12

the room, and the crowded bar opened up to welcome them, Steve's money ignored as Big Terry stood ready for their order.

'A pint for you, eh, Bernie?' he said. 'An' what you 'aving, Roy?'

Roy's mouth puckered slightly and the entire bar seemed to want to wait for his answer.

'Yeah, that'll do for me,' he said, staring right through the guv'nor.

And then, with the brothers there and the drinks coming up, everything seemed to be in order at last and a murmur of quiet, preoccupied conversation began.

Steve stood silent. He couldn't bear to start on diamond rings again, not even for the look of it, so he got in with his order, doubling it up, and he leaned there showing himself for Bernie to see, ready to be called over for a talk.

It took about an hour: the tenner was nearly gone and he was beginning not to give a damn anyway when a small group moved away from the bar and Bernie suddenly pitched his voice up a bit and said, ' 'Ello, Stevie, son; 'evening, Val; glad you made it. . . .'

'Oh, you're welcome, Bernie.' Val's smile showed her small white teeth; but there was no lift to the corners of her mouth. 'Cheers, Roy. . . .'

Roy was leaning on the bar behind his brother, his eyes heavy-hooded with boredom, his pock-textured skin and beaked nose adding to the impression of a resting bird of prey. He raised his glass a fraction in response, but nothing of his face moved.

'What you drinking, Steve?' Bernie took his glass and sniffed. 'Terry, a brandy for Steve here. And whatever the lady's 'aving. . . .' He waited while the drinks were poured, saying nothing, but staring at Steve in an appraising sort of way. Then, as Steve sipped, he smiled: the perfect moment to make his move, as always, whether it was sweet talk or a swift kick. 'Now then, Stevie, all the lads will definitely want to know you've come to tell me what I want to hear. . . .'

13

Bernie was firmly in charge now, acting as if he were the managing director bringing on a shy young executive, even to the gold-rimmed glasses he casually put on to examine more closely one of the pound notes he'd been given in his change.

Steve folded his arms and nursed his brandy like a pint tankard; and he nodded. 'Yeah. 'Course, Bernie. Never no doubt, was there . . . ?'

'Well done, Stevie. A good decision, eh, Roy? You won't be sorry, son.' Bernie put both his hands flat on the bar and leaned over them, drawing Steve in closer to hear what he was going to say. 'Only I need a good driver in a fast motor who knows all the back doubles round the ground. . . .' His voice was flat and fairly quiet. 'City East. The Arsenal game in a fortnight. We're doin' a special job at the end of the second 'alf, just before the whistle goes.' He smiled at the simple ingenuity of his plan. 'Only, if we time it right an' you drive out the car park a minute or so before full-time, no one'll know which bloody way you've gone, the lads'll get lost in the crowd, an' the 'ole place'll grind to an 'alt for a good twenty minutes. . . .'

Steve stared at him and sipped his brandy. He nodded with the slight exaggeration of the drink. 'Yeah, sounds all right,' he said. 'Yeah. Do a left out the ground, left at the Woodman, and get lost round the back doubles off Kath'rine Road. Park down one of them darkie streets an' leave it there for a couple of hours. They won't look for it down there. Something like that. No trouble.' He finished his drink.

'Good boy, Stevie. Lovely, son, you're thinking. Eh, Roy?' Bernie turned to get his brother to share in the approval.

'Yeah,' said Roy without enthusiasm. 'A real treat.'

'Great! So I'll be in touch, with all the details,' Bernie said, taking the empty glass out of Steve's hand and setting it down for a refill. And while Steve followed it with his eyes and smiled, Bernie winked, speed-of-light fast at Val: and she smiled, quickly, at the older Bradshaw. And this time her eyes sparkled, and she allowed the corners of her mouth to lift slightly.

2

Ronnie frowned when his father put it to him later. Just not understanding, and the strong suspicion that it was the brandy talking, not Steve, put what Val called his thick look on his face. But it *was* hard to grasp, because nothing like this had ever happened before.

'Well, what d'you say, son, yes or no? D'you wanna come or don't you?'

Eh? Ronnie frowned harder and he rocked forward slightly as if he were hard of hearing. But it wasn't his ears. His brain just couldn't sort out this jumble of totally new ideas.

Steve said it again, slower. 'Saturday week, City East versus the Arsenal. You wanna come with me, up in the box, special tickets, don't you? Eh? You an' me? Up in the posh seats . . . ?' He rubbed his hands to induce excitement, and he swayed slightly.

Ronnie's face began to clear. Yeah, he was getting it now. But him and his dad weren't footballers, or football fans; and although they sometimes had a good laugh at the telly, they hardly ever went anywhere together. So he was still a bit bewildered inside as he shrugged his shoulders and muttered, 'If you like. . . .'

'Well, don' get too excited, boy,' Steve said as he went out to the kitchen. He put his arm round Val's small waist.

' "If you like," he said; "If you like"!' Steve gave her a
sardonic smile and a squeeze. But she didn't react to him.
She was busy in a mirror, pulling off a long line of eye-lash.

Ronnie sat in the wide passenger seat with the look and the
life of a rag doll, his legs stiff in new jeans and stuck straight
out in front of him, his arms hanging limp at his sides. Only
the slight frown on his white face showed that behind the
thick mask, beneath the red and white bobble hat, his mind
was active and aware; as switched-on as it always had to be.
    The car was stolen, he knew that. It made no difference.
It was just a fact, no more a matter for question than where
the apple in his pocket had come from—Israel or South
Africa: an apple was an apple and a car was a car. Except
this one was big. This one was a real motor. It was old-
fashioned and black and padded and quiet, with a sliding
panel above their heads to let in the sun, when it was sunny.
But on that chilly March day Steve had the heater on, and
he sat there next to Ronnie in the slow-moving traffic shivering a bit, and tapping his big ring on the steering wheel, his
mouth tensing and relaxing, sighing through his clenched
teeth. Ronnie knew it was no normal outing with his dad,
this. For a start it wasn't normal to be going out. No,
this was all part of something else, something to do with
Bradshaw coming round and talking about City East. And
he didn't like it any more now than he had before.
    But if you were going to football, this was the way to do
it: never mind parking a mile away and walking like all these
others; just drive on past them and up to the main gates of
the ground.
    'Ere y'are,' said Steve. 'Show 'im this.' He put his hand
inside his brown leather coat and pulled out a large white
card. 'City East Football Club,' it said on it. 'Guest Ticket.
Admit Two.' But to Ronnie it was just a piece of card;
perhaps instead of money, he thought. The car stopped
between the gates of the car park, and a man in commission-

aire's uniform was waiting to check the card. Ronnie worked the window and showed it to him.

'Thank you very much, sir. On your left.'

The car purred smoothly in and with a show of nonchalant expertise Steve stopped it with its nose against a wire mesh fence in the car park. Ronnie got out, slammed the door, and waited for his dad to do the same; but Steve didn't; instead, he hung his head out of the window and waved Ronnie up to him. His voice was low and urgent.

'Now, for God's sake don't make a bloody great fuss about it, but you see over there against the wall, them orange beer crates in that space?' Ronnie nodded. 'Now, walk over an' look like you're meant to do it, an' stack 'em out the way round the corner.' He looked past Ronnie to where more big cars were cruising in like yachts to moorings. 'An' don't let no one in that space but me, right?'

Ronnie said nothing. So he *was* part of whatever this was all about. He hadn't just been brought along for the ride. He sniffed, and nodded, and without question he went over to the crates and did as he was told, closely followed by Steve in the car, who reversed smoothly all the way to glide into the space at the end of the building, a place on its own, partly hidden by a high brick wall. Steve got out, and looked up.

The tall building, the back of the west grandstand, stretched across in front of them like a huge factory and from inside the corrugated arena beyond came the hoarse chants of rival spectators already locked in conflict. The floodlights were already partly on against the grey afternoon, and an atmosphere of unreal excitement curled in the air with the tobacco smoke. But Ronnie's narrowed eyes were on the crinkly squares of light which shone out from the various offices high above their heads.

'Come on,' said Steve. 'Stop day-dreaming. Up in the posh seats....'

They took their places next to the gangway in row H.

They upped and downed a few times for cigars, fur coats, and loud voices to sidle past, and then while Steve pretended an interest in the programme, looking round casually for the positions of the law and a glimpse of a familiar face, Ronnie let his mind play despondently on what this afternoon was all about.

It was all about being scared, for a start. This was all Bradshaw's business, there'd been no secret about that; him and his dad were both part of a plan which the brothers had set up; and the nerves in his stomach were telling him, as they'd told him for a fortnight, that that could only mean trouble; more reason than ever for being scared. Now there was going to be a new reason for no one saying anything out of place, a new reason for months of tingling down his spine. 'Load of stupid berks, the lot!' Ronnie said to himself: and even he wasn't sure whether he meant the villains' world he lived in or the whole of the stupid human race.

Forty thousand others chanted or read their programmes or chattered until the teams came out. But Steve and Ronnie Webster just sat and stared silently into space: Steve in contemplation of what he had to do, and Ronnie in puzzlement of what it might be. Was it drugs? Or hot jewellery? Was someone sitting close-by going to pass something on to Steve—a packet or an envelope or something? Or was it money? Were they going to help nick all that money pouring in? (That was favourite, Ronnie thought. Something to do with those offices). Or perhaps it was revenge? Was this a grudge matter, when someone here got done on behalf of the Bradshaws? Were they going to drive off with a body in the back of that big motor? It had been known: one or two *had* disappeared round here. Or it might be a kidnap, with one of the players getting bundled into the big boot. He didn't know and he daren't ask: so in the end, his mind saturated with all the things it might turn out to be, he shut his ears to the shouts and his eyes to the crowd's swaying movement, and he leant forward, rocking a bit, resting his arms on his knees and staring with his sightless eyes at the floor. Sometimes there was just too much to take in and you had to shut the lot out....

Ronnie looked up for a bit when the teams ran out, and he followed some of the backwards and forwards movements of the white ball. But like so many of the hours in school this one was spent in just waiting for the end of it to come and for the next thing to begin. The difference was, while the end of school might mean a fast and frightened run home, from here today the end was going to lead to something bigger, something much more definite—whatever it turned out to be.

All around him he could see everyone going mad; and in a sing-song voice, Steve told him why. 'No goals, you see, son; not yet anyhow; and they need these two points desperate. Arsenal need 'em to put 'em in reach of the championship; and City East need 'em to avoid the drop—relegation. See?' The boy's face was still blank, but it didn't matter, the excitement was enough. For Steve it couldn't be better. Every run, every tackle, every clash in the air, was triggering off its own nervous spasm of sound. The oval arena was like a loud open mouth. If this kept up no one would hear a thing. Or see it. They were all too riveted on the game. Even the club officials, normally too busy behind the scenes to show an interest, were crowding the tunnels as the game tussled towards an end, and caterers were gawping out from under their shuttered bars.

Steve looked at his watch. Was that the time already? Then it was all happening now. Downstairs. The game had come and gone in front of them; and now, down the office, the lads were busy. Four more minutes and he and the boy would have to leave their seats. The last lap had come so quickly! He inflated his cheeks and blew out and he looked round at Ronnie. He'd done well, the boy. They'd looked the part—father and son at the football. Now if only the kid could keep his head when it happened it'd all end up perfect....

Precisely six minutes earlier the first stage had already ended perfectly in the Secretary's office above the car park. The takings had been counted, bundled and sorted into piles ready for its final bagging-up and for the short journey after the match to the night-safe down the road. The Secretary's secret knock had been given; but when the door had been opened four Security men had burst into the office, shouting and jabbing shot-guns and determination at the heads of the cashiers. And in just three minutes the turnstile takings had been heaped in six sacks in the middle of the floor, with a seventh standing handy on a table by the window. Perfect. No one had been touched. One of the clerks had tried to squirt aerosol dye on the money to mark it—but he'd missed the notes and he'd dropped the can when he'd seen how determined the raiders were. Now, with nervous blinks, the cashiers watched the visored faces of the gunmen for some sign that might tell them what their fate would be. Would they be coshed? Or a hostage taken? And which one of them if there was? Or would they all just be tied up and sellotaped into silence? But from behind their smoked face-shields the gang gave nothing away. Only the man by the door, concentrating on the stop-watch on his wrist, revealed what was in their minds. It was all a matter of time. Clearly their timing needed to be as split-second accurate as the referee's.

Steve Webster looked urgently down at the time pulsing on his own wrist. He looked up again. With seconds to go the crowd was in a frenzy of excitement. Fighting had broken out behind the north goal, and all around the skirmish a sea of red and white bobbed in rhythm to an obscene chant while a dozen policemen ran to the centre. Nil–nil, and the match was at flash-point: every pair of eyes was focused either on the bright green rectangle of pitch or on the terrace fighting. The police were up to their helmets in aggravation.

It was a perfect set-up for a snatch.

Steve's seat banged as he got up; but only Ronnie noticed. 'Come on, son,' he said, all normal. 'Time to go. Beat the crowds.' He pulled Ronnie's arm, and together, suddenly no longer bothering to pretend an interest in the game, they hurried towards the stairs and, half-walking, half-running, and jumping whole flights as they neared the bottom, they swung round the pillars and accelerated towards the car.

Ronnie ran hard behind, head twisting over his shoulder as usual, but he was pretty sure now that whatever they'd come for had been done, and now they were getting away. It had been easy, he thought. Dead easy. But they weren't home yet....

More relaxed now that the action had begun, Steve opened the driver's door and slid into the seat, and almost in one smooth movement he adjusted the choke and started the quiet engine. Then he leaned over and opened up the front passenger door for Ronnie. He smiled. It had been almost as smooth as the old running start at Le Mans, he thought.

Ronnie sat in and started sniffing in the felt-lined gloom, sniffing impatiently while Steve checked his watch and switched on the interior light. The reflection of a cold drawn face was thrown on to the windscreen, and it took a full second for Ronnie to realize who it was. It was him under that stupid woollen hat. He sat and stared himself out, waiting for the jolt in his back and the spurt to the gate, the stuff his dad was good at. But it didn't come; instead Steve was fiddling about beside him, opening the sunshine roof. What the hell was going on?

'Keep your 'ead out the way!' Steve commanded. 'Some stuff's comin' down. When it does, sling it down be'ind the seat and then sit up straight an' read your programme. Well, pretend. An' try an' look interested in it . . . as if nothing was going on, right?' He pulled the match programme out of Ronnie's pocket and tossed it to him. Then he got out of the car and began a lengthy adjustment of the wing mirror on the driver's side; but all the while his eyes were flicking his real interest around the car park and up above him—on the small rectangle of yellow light from the office.

So far, so good, Steve thought. The stadium builders could have planned this lay-out with the Bradshaws in mind. Parked there beneath the office the car was conveniently masked from the police at the gate by the corner of a high brick wall. So when the light went out above him and the window opened it would be hard to see anything happening as the darkened mail-bags dropped towards the lighted target in the car roof. The near-misses would be swept in like lightning and he'd be away ahead of the crowd before word even got out that the gate money had been hit.

Ronnie, blinking caution, turned his face up into the black draught. He saw the small window fifteen metres above: and at that moment, suddenly, he saw it all. Yeah! Too true! He'd been right. It *was* going to be money—coming down from up there. All the pound notes people paid to get in, dropping down into the motor. God, that was why he'd got to look normal! To cover up for that! He backed his head out of the line of the drop and opened the programme, anywhere, on to a page dense with meaningless words; but that didn't matter, he wasn't looking at it: his mind was too full with something else now.

Worry again. Real fear. He'd guessed it, but now he knew it for certain. His dad *had* gone and done it again. He'd dropped him in it again, right in it again, right over his head with the Bradshaws. He found himself fighting a feeling of sickness and the strangling grip of not being able to breathe properly. His forehead pricked with sweat beneath the bobble-hat. Oh, God! There had always been a skinny chance that Steve wouldn't be too much in it, a bit of hope to hold on to right up to the final finding out. But now he knew. It was all starting all over again, for definite....

After the third re-positioning of the wing-mirror Steve swore and pressed at the button on his wrist again. 16.41.

Come on! It had to be done by now! They were a minute late up there, and this timing was supposed to be split-second. His job was to just beat the crowd, not get caught up in it, getting stopped and searched like an idiot. Come on, for God's sake! He looked round anxiously. One or two more people were coming down from the grandstand to the car park. Inside the stadium the crowd had gone quiet, and it was clear the match was already an anticlimax: there wouldn't be any more goals, and the interest had gone after all the high hopes. The number of early leavers was grow-ing, and any second now that whistle would go and all hell would be let loose. He checked his watch again. 16.41 and forty seconds. Come on! Come on! He looked up again. Still that light was on. Still no sign of anything happening. He pulled a couple of tissues out of his pocket and rubbed the clean windscreen vigorously.

Perhaps they hadn't made it up there. Perhaps it had all gone wrong. Well, things definitely weren't right, were they? he thought. Perhaps it'd be favourite to forget this cock-up and clear off in the car. Yeah. He put his hand on the door catch—and immediately snatched it off again as if it were burning hot. God, no! Not likely! He couldn't do that! He'd be the biggest prize idiot in London to do that! He'd make a nice heap of blood and guts up some back alley if he did that. You didn't clear off out from under the Bradshaws and then stay in one piece to show it could be done. No way. Even if it meant going down, you went down. There were worse things than going to prison. Steve knew that, just as Ronnie knew there were worse things than going to school. So he went on polishing the windscreen, his hand jerking in short, anxious, rubs. Just as long as they didn't start chucking the stuff down after the whistle went. That was all he asked now.

The whistle went. Inside the stadium the referee gave three long blasts to a played-out cheer from the crowd. 16.42. Bang on time. And at that moment one of the bags came out of the office window. Cutting it bloody fine! Steve thought, as it was held suspended. He stood on his toes, waiting for them all to come flopping down. And put that light out! But the light stayed on, the window swung further out, and a visored head appeared.

'We got problems,' it shouted hoarsely. 'Get this one away! We'll settle for this one!' And then down it came, white instead of black, flying and flapping in the reflected light like a wounded swan. 'Go on!' the voice repeated from the window, as if Steve were some sort of imbecile who didn't understand. 'Get off with that!'

The sack landed on the car roof with a noise loud enough to be a body. Inside, Ronnie jumped in his seat and hurt his elbow on the arm rest.

Already Steve was moving, swearing as he went. God alive, the whole of Shepherds Gate must've seen and heard that. Now he'd got to move so fast it wasn't true. With a wide sweep of his arm he sent the sack in through the sunshine roof, and he leapt into the car and had it moving before the sack had bounced off the back seat and settled on the floor.

'Light!' he yelled. 'Put the bloody light out!'

If Steve had had time to feel proud, or had ever known what it was to feel pride in his son, he'd have felt it then. Despite the hard stiffness of his new jeans, Ronnie was up on his seat and frisking his hands down the door columns within three seconds; and when he couldn't find what he was groping for there he quickly worked out which was the only likely switch on the dashboard and switched it off. Meanwhile, Steve, with both hands on the top of the wheel, was already up to forty in his race to be at the head of the cars which would be stringing out of the car park any second. He knew just what he had to do. He'd been in this sort of situation before, on the race track, and this afternoon he knew that if anyone could get a car two metres wide through a gap closing quickly to one and a half, it was Steve Webster. And that was what he was going to have to do, because people were shouting, a whistle was blowing, and in his headlights he could see a uniformed policeman moving to-wards him.

Steve quickly decided he didn't need to hit-and-run to get past the man. That wasn't his style anyway. And the man didn't look all that determined. While his mind was waking up to the possibility of a wages snatch his body was still on traffic duty, and there was nothing do-or-die about him yet. With a controlled two-handed flick to the left, which he'd corrected almost before he'd made it, Steve swept the car to the policeman's right, a few centimetres of rushing air between the car and the man's tunic buttons, and with his horn blaring out a scare the ex-racing driver headed for the gate, the crucial left bend he had to take in front of the rest—or be boxed in and pulled up by the law.

On each side of his squealing course angry men pulled back their sons, a fist thumped on the roof of the car, and a dumpy woman, all scarlet mouth and horn-rims, shrieked abuse on behalf of them all. But Steve saw hardly any of that. His attention was on a red Maxi coming in fast from the right, the car he had to beat to the gate to get away. He pinked the engine into an incapable rattle as his foot pressed for more than it could give; but the big vehicle picked up quickly and the metres began to disappear beneath it like Essex under an air liner. The exit gate came at them. Now it suddenly depended as much on the other driver as on Steve. As they were both going, with the Maxi a fraction closer to the gate, Steve knew the man might decide to be awkward and put on a spurt to balk him; or on the other hand he might chicken out of scratching his wing and give way. Well, dents and scratches wouldn't bother Steve; no way: and because Steve had nothing to lose there was only one thing he could do. He had to get through, by superior speed, or skill, or force: but at any cost he had to get through. It was the sort of decision a racing driver made ten times a lap, a decision based on his knowledge of his superior ability under stress. It was only when the other man was as sure as he was that trouble came.

''Old on!' Steve shouted. And he went for the left hand post of the gate, his body back in a relaxed line as his foot pressed hard to the floor and the car leapt at the waving commissionaire. It was like a road accident. The Maxi owner suddenly threw his brakes on so hard his passenger almost went through the windscreen, and the accumulated mud and rust from under the wheel arches showered the tarmac as if he'd crashed. The commissionaire threw himself aside with a leap twenty years younger, while with a screech of its tyres the Daimler crossed the pavement and careered into Shepherds Lane on the near-side, racing for the Woodman lights. There'd be no half-measures. They'd get away or they wouldn't. Pedestrians and cars jumped and swerved as Steve bumped back up on the pavement to get inside the line and he raced to the head of the slowing queue at the corner.

So far, so good. But this was crucial, this bit. This was the whole point of using a crack driver. Steve knew it, and so did Ronnie. Close behind them the sinister wail of a siren wound itself up. Steve had to prove his worth now. He had to move fast or the departing crowd—huge enough to jam up anyone following—would start to get so dense no one in it would be able to move out of Steve's way quickly enough to save their own lives.

Steve seemed reckless. He ran the car at groups and clusters, bluffing injury, but really judging distances to the centimetre; and with a last desperate spurt, by sheer steering skill and speed and one hundred per cent determination, he made it first to the corner and with a sweep of his practised arms took a hard, tight, left over the red lights. He ignored the oncoming bulk of a number fifteen bus, skimming the high bonnet like a skate-board across the front of a pram, and he tail-spun into the Barking Road as if it were a race track lined with bales of straw.

Ronnie gripped the fascia desperately, eyes staring, mouth open, like someone on the Big Dipper. His dad always drove fast, but never like this, not in traffic, not up and down off the bloody pavement! There'd be a crash. They'd be killed, both of them. If it wasn't a berk in another car it'd be a lamp-post, or a shop front.... And yet somehow it was all unreal, like a dream, almost as if he were outside himself looking on. For a second he took his eyes off the Barking Road and stared at Steve. Steve was sitting back, his arms out straight before him, his leather hands at ten and two on the wheel, adjusting, refining, flipping left and right, his face a mask, relaxed without a visible trace of tension; calmly, almost hypnotically, pushing his car on and away from the trapped wail behind them. And with that power pushing into Ronnie's back, too, the motion, the same hypnotism of things rushing at him, it suddenly didn't matter a toss to Ronnie if they *did* crash. Shoot through the windscreen, die, it was all part of this forward thrust, all part of this screaming towards something....

'Come on, 'old on, I said!'

Ronnie's eyes glazed again now, turned emotionless back to the fascia as he obediently pushed himself against it. Like this, he'd do anything he was told.

He held on just in time. Suddenly Steve threw the wheel to the left, leaning into Ronnie, his near hand out and gripping the door beyond him, as he slewed the car at speed on to the far pavement of Priors Road; then a bump, a swerve, a deep howl from the tyres as they were snaked out straight, and they headed up towards the back streets behind the stadium. And only now, as they slowed down, did Ronnie's stomach begin to roll again with slow fear; now, just as Steve reduced his speed and broke the boy's trance, as all at once he became the model driver in the darkened streets.

He took a right turn, two lefts and another right; he indicated correctly, positioned well, flashed his headlights to give right of way; and then he stopped, applying the hand-brake with a long and deliberate ratcheting of the mechanism. He closed the open roof, checked the rear-view mirror again, and, like the man over the road coming home from work, he got out of the car and meticulously locked up on his side. Steve walked round to Ronnie's door and opened it.

'Come on,' he said. 'We've lost 'em. Now we're walkin'. . . .'

Ronnie got out and stood still facing the nearest house while Steve took out the match programme from the floor, wiped both the fascia and the steering wheel with a gloved hand, and put the rear mats over the single mail bag in the back. Then he locked Ronnie's door and, after a couple of careful glances up and down the street, he went to the front of the car.

One swift rip took off the false adhesive number-plate like a plaster off a cut, and a similar swift action followed at the back. He balled up the tacky fistful and rammed it into his pocket.

'They'll think we're down Southend by now,' he said. 'That's done 'em. . . .' and he led off down the dark street.

Ronnie made a funny noise in his throat.

'Do what?' said Steve; but he wasn't interested. He'd still got a lot on his mind. He'd done his bit, hadn't he? But all that yelling at the window, and only one sack! There wasn't going to be much to come back and pick up when the heat was off.

Ronnie swallowed, and scowled, and gurgled again in his throat. But he didn't say anything. Because he couldn't. Because how did you tell someone what he'd just seen? Something that could make a disaster of the whole thing? A face at the window of the house by the car: a familiar face: a shy but nosy face round the curtain: Manjit Mirza from Miss Lessor's group at school. Someone who'd been watching him as sure as eggs was eggs.

Ronnie stumbled along behind his father. Stupid thick

28

girl! She would! Silly black cow! She'd give the whole stinking thing away! Oh God! What the hell could he about her? He looked sideways, suspicious, from under lowered lids.

And then the itching down his back told him there was really only one thing he could do. What the others did. His eyes widened in the dark, and his body suddenly felt light as he began to experience, there in the back street, what it felt like to be one of them—beginning to think the same sort of crippling threats as the Bradshaws....

3

Ash from a small cigar fell into the typewriter cradle. It danced as the letters of 'assault' were struck, before disintegrating into the mechanism. Detective Inspector Johnnie Kingsland squinted at what he'd got on paper so far.

'This Smith's a right tastie,' he said to the room in general. 'Georgie Knights stops Smith's van outside the docks, and in the back there's only nine of our Indian friends in sleeping-bags. Smith says, "I don't know how they got there. They must have got in at the traffic lights. . . ."! What a defence! Typical! The law's just a game to some of these characters. . . .'

There were a couple of preoccupied grunts and a long pause. Then, 'Yeah. Never mind, guv. We can still do Smith for hiding Sikh!' D.C. Jones laughed explosively at his own wit. 'Ha! "Hiding Sikh!" I'll give that to the *Mercury* for a headline. Must be worth a drink when the Immigration boys get him into court. . . .'

But his play on words went unacknowledged. In the C.I.D.

office it was difficult enough for words to be fixed to paper, to be made to stick, for them to be appreciated flying lightly about in the air: incidents could be funny, or people: but rarely words. Too much depended on them.

The telephone rang on the desk Detective Inspector Kingsland was using.

'D.I.' His smoked eyes squinted at the desk while he listened. After a few seconds he put the receiver down and stubbed his cigar out in a saucer.

'City East!' he said, scraping to his feet. 'There goes the week-end! Come on, they've done the gate money. Chris, you hang on here.' He buttoned his waistcoat and slid into his suit jacket, instantly smart. The rest of the office rose as a man and followed the tall D.I. out to the cars.

'It's the Bradshaws, guv. It's got to be....'

'Yeah, all smiles and alibis....'

'Barratt's gonna look a twit. He had more helmets at the ground than a miners' gala....'

Fifteen minutes had the C.I.D. clustered inside the secretary's office while their uniformed colleagues questioned stragglers at the gate. Chief Superintendent Barratt was out on the pitch doing an interview down the line to London Weekend Television, who had been covering the match. He was stalling, confident answers straight to camera, trying to give nothing of his ignorance away. Meanwhile, D.I. Kingsland was finding out what had gone on, and before the white television lights had switched Mr. Barratt off, the detective was summing it up for the shocked cashiers.

'So, five of them were let in after giving the usual security signal, all of them dressed like Security men in tinted helmets and blue jackets. They all carried shot guns, which they threatened you with, and they tied you up with sticky tape. Then they took the money you'd counted and put the notes and bags of fifty p.'s inside their raincoats in rows of special pockets.' Kingsland's eyes followed the reported movements as he described them. He looked at the small window. 'They threw one bag out there, one man shouted out at someone below, and then the five of them dumped their helmets in the corner and walked out of the door, looking like ordinary spectators leaving the ground....'

The heads nodded. It all sounded so simple, the way he put it, as if they'd just given in.

'Simple, wasn't it?' Johnnie Kingsland knew how simple it always was, and how difficult it always was for the police. It was a matter of a second to knock beer on the floor, a lifetime to get over its presence in the best carpet. He singled out the woman. Women sometimes noticed things men didn't. 'So they came in wearing the helmets, and they went out wearing the raincoats. They took things off and put things on in here....'

'They made us turn our backs when they'd taken the helmets off. They said they'd shoot anyone who turned round. *Shoot!* We didn't even dare to have a go with the dye. They were too vicious. George had a quick squirt at some of the money, but he dropped the can when he saw they meant what they said—didn't you, George?'

George shrugged helplessly, and nodded. He had a wife and two young children.

'Yes, it must've been quite an ordeal.' The detective picked up the small can of indelible spray: a tell-tale dye to use on money and a useful defence against half-hearted assailants who would be frightened off by the thought of carrying a bright purple mark on their skin that wouldn't wash away for a year. He turned to the young man who'd had half a go with it. 'You sprayed one of them? Or any of the money?'

'Sorry, mate, but would you?' he asked, defensive. 'I gave one of 'em a quick squirt, but he took it on his rubber glove, and then I dropped it. Anyhow, a drip of bloody paint's no good against a shot-gun!'

'Yes, sure. You did right. They're illegal now, anyway, but you did right.' Kingsland turned back to the woman.

'But fiddling with chin straps and raincoat buttons and handling the money: they needed fingers for that, bare hands: now, love, was there anything about their hands—rings, tattoos, bracelets, marks....?' He ran his own fingers back through his receding hairline.

'Rubber gloves,' she said quickly. 'Like George said. All of them. The first thing I noticed....'

Kingsland sighed and rubbed his red eyes. Already his scene-of-crime officer was measuring the room before going over its surface for prints, and D.C. Jones was putting the helmets into plastic bags. But there wouldn't be anything. And now the long grind of statement-taking lay ahead. 'Yes, very simple: and there'll be nothing here. Helmets stolen months ago, shot-guns taken from a gunsmith who'll swear he never owned them. Not much of an outlay for today's gate. So, what have we got?' He gave the impression of thinking aloud, but he'd done that ten minutes before: now he just fed in ideas with his quiet Camberwell voice. 'They spoke, so we've got the voices. . . .' A pause while it registered. A flicker from one of them? A blink? 'And we've got a description of that decoy car under the window....' Stop again, eyes worrying at the room, frowning over the restless witnesses. There was plenty to tell, wasn't there? 'But on the surface, not a lot. Till something turns up....'

None of the policemen looked very confident about that; but they all knew Kingsland's style: he hadn't said it, but he clearly thought there was someone—an inside man or woman—who knew a lot about this: perhaps someone in the room now: and Kingsland would work on that. He was good on theories and facts and physical clues, this man, but he was brilliant on people. And once he got going on the likely inside man, he wouldn't give up till he'd cracked him. They watched him as he unwrapped a strip of gum and nibbled it into his mouth. His typical style was to strike up a really sympathetic relationship, something matey and warm, but all the time he'd be working for his own professional ends.

It was Kingsland's strength, the friendliness and patience which masked his determination to get results.

The D.I. turned to the woman. 'Live far away?' he asked, straightening his tie.

It was easier to drift along on the current of routine than to strike out against it, especially when you had as little confidence as Ronnie. On the Monday morning after the match he shuffled into Miss Lessor's tiny reading room just as he always did, and as usual he sat down without any sign of expression on his face. But today his routine attendance concealed another purpose—a purpose about as vague and unformed as any of his doings—and his downcast eyes held a serious stare at Manjit Mirza which was secret from Miss Lessor.

Miss Lessor was in an irritable Monday mood.

'Right, Ronnie,' she said, leaving Manjit to sound out 'Sally at Home' in unfamiliar intonations. 'Show me how you've been getting on with those cards I gave you.' She tapped a hard finger-nail on the table where the cards were to be spread out. But her unfocused eyes showed that she wasn't really with him; and the specialness of Ronnie was absent from her tone today: so when he reached in his pocket and brought out the cards bent and torn her exasperation quickly surfaced.

'Oh, really, Ronnie! Just look at them! Is that any way to treat the apparatus?'

Ronnie scowled. Get stuffed! Stuff the rotten cards. He couldn't care less about cards. . . .

Frowning, Miss Lessor scooped them from him and tried to press them back flat; but they'd been bent too much by the way they'd been treated and they wouldn't have it: they were too far gone. She sighed. She was really annoyed.

'They're not all here, anyway. Are they?'

A quick glance at the odd number on the table showed that at least one of the cards was missing.

'That means I'm going to have to make you some more—and it's your learning time you're wasting while I do it. *I* don't care. *I* can read and write!' She got up. 'And you won't take these home to lose again, boy. Now sit and do what you can with the old ones while I get the card to cut; and you can say sorry to Manjit for wasting *her* time too....'

She picked up her handbag and went from the room, leaving Manjit reading the unfamiliar sentences and Ronnie scowling at the cardboard.

A landing below the stock cupboard door banged open.

They were alone. Ronnie looked up. He didn't reckon in minutes or anything—he never had—but he guessed he'd just about got time to do what he'd been thinking about since Saturday.

The car had been found, he knew that. It had been on the news over the week-end, with all the other details of the headline-making raid. But they didn't know who'd been driving it: and right from the first second he'd seen her looking out from behind that curtain he'd known he had to make sure this black kid kept her mouth shut. Tight! And he had to do it. It was no good trying to tell his dad. He'd just sat and drunk since Saturday night, useless; but even so, as much as the drink curled his mouth round foul and hateful words, Ronnie knew he'd settle for that any day than for an empty chair, with Steve in prison. So he had to do it.

Now, like a cat leaning forward in attack, Ronnie was growling deep in his throat without knowing it. It was the only sound he made, because he didn't know what to say. It was impossible to put into words what he wanted. Like his mother writing a rare note, he didn't know how to begin. He got up and went towards the girl, scowling, searching round in his mind for the right words that'd make her listen and take a bit of notice. But still he couldn't think of what to say. The growl became a louder, conscious, snarl: and still she wouldn't look up: still her head was stuck into that

34

stupid book, saying it out all foreign and sing-song.

The stupid black cow! She needn't come this stupid reading rubbish with him. This was too bloody important! He looked round at the door.

Then he kicked her.

It wasn't a soft warning of what might come. It was a hard kick aimed at her calf, and as his foot struck she cried out; and as she shrieked he found the pressure holding back his words suddenly released.

'You keep your mouth shut, right?'

Manjit drew back, her face screwed up, her hand clutching her leg; but the kick had hit the chair leg as well as the calf, and there was as much surprise as pain in her reaction. How did he mean, keep her mouth shut? The shout she made? Or the reading out? Or was this just another kick for nothing? her look asked.

'You know! Me an' my dad . . . Sat'day!' The idiot Paki cow, pulling that stupid face. She bloody knew.

Saturday. Yes, she'd seen him on Saturday. But why . . . ? What difference did that make? Her leg hurt, and she was still unsure. Anger welled up in her, but she was too afraid to show it. 'Why?' she asked.

He hit her: a hard knuckly punch on the muscle of her arm, numbing it, making her lose her grip on her book. She screamed, and shrieked a fierce stream of outraged Punjabi, her eyes on fire, her plaited hair shaking down.

'You know!' Ronnie's face was screwed up at her, his own eyes blazing out with the threats his mouth didn't. Yeah, she knew why all right! If she saw him getting out of the car, and then the police came and took it off, she must know why she'd got to keep her trap shut. Everyone knew why when Bernie Bradshaw did the threatening, so she must know why with him.

But Ronnie had gone too far. He'd misjudged it, a thing Bernie Bradshaw would never do. Now he'd made her cry; loudly, unstoppably, and instead of making sure of her silence he'd made sure of her pained, complaining, noise. There was more to being a Bradshaw than landing out with dead-arms and kickings....

'You spiteful little beast! What foul hole did you crawl out from this morning?' Miss Lessor banged him hard over the head with a packet of thick card. 'Hitting girls! I saw that! Get out! Go on, get down to your class, and tell Miss Neame why I've sent you back. You horrible little thug!' She threw the packet of cards on to the table with a crack and stood aside to let him pass her in the narrow room. He ducked, and fled quickly, and she had to call her parting words after him.

'I just hope for your sake Manjit's father doesn't come up to complain....'

Ronnie, round the corner, slowed to a slouch; and from the room he'd left he heard, in the common language of the girl's crying, a sudden increase in its volume before it was hushed.

Johnnie Kingsland walked out through the three-man-wide back door which led from the police cells to the station yard. D.C. Jones, the wordy one, followed him, stopping when the D.I. stopped on the steps.

'It's like Battersea Dogs' Home with all these cars,' said Jones.

Kingsland frowned. What the hell was Jonesey on about now?

'Eh, guv? All lost, stolen, or strayed. Fords like mongrels, and that sleek black Daimler like a thoroughbred greyhound....'

Kingsland licked the palm of his hand and flattened a flyaway wisp of thinning hair with it. 'Have you got that key?' he asked.

'Crumpled wings like bitten ears....'

'The key, Shakespeare?'

'Oh, yes. Here....' Jones handed over the labelled key

which belonged to the black greyhound, Steve's hot motor.

D.I. Kingsland walked all round it as it stood exhibit-still there in the yard: lifeless now, like a corpse. But it wasn't an appraising look he gave it; more puzzled, a worried frown. He bent his tall lean frame, prodded the windows with his sharp nose as he squinted inside. To Jones he looked like an inquisitive rook.

'You know, it's funny, Jonesey,' he said, 'we got one sack out of this about as fat as Christmas post in August, less than a hundred quid all told. And there's hardly any petrol in the tank—so it wasn't going very far, and its driver knew it wasn't. Once it was nicked there was no sense risking a long stand at the pumps. So, if it wasn't meant for the get-away, why throw out a thin sack? If they were doing the decoy thing, why didn't they make it look really good and at least fill the back seat with full sacks, stuffed with news-paper or something?'

Jones, stroking a Datsun, thought for a minute. 'Well, perhaps it was just to throw *something* down, guv. Someone yelled out of the window, so they definitely wanted anyone who happened to be in the car park to take notice. . . .'

'Then why sling out any money at all?' Kingsland hadn't looked round at him. His grey eyes were only for the car. 'Why not sling out telephone books in a sack, something at least looking a bit like a sack of loot? Why just a few quid in a flat sack that anyone could have mistaken for a big pigeon dropping down dead?' Kingsland stood back. 'No, Jonesey, I'm just wondering who they were trying to fool. . . .' He went back to the driver's door. 'Who searched the vehicle Saturday night?'

'Me. I did, guv.' Jones's proud and confident voice tried to let the inspector know he'd made a good job of it. Well, he *had* done a good job, and by torchlight.

'Right,' said Kingsland, 'well, apologies: but you never know. Chummy might have slipped up somewhere. And it's always best to check by daylight.'

'Sure, guv. Be my guest.' The distrusting so-and-so, thought Jones. Well, search on. You won't find anything. He didn't interfere; he stood back and watched the D.I. work; but he couldn't help admiring the way his guv'nor gave the car the once-over. It was a real professional job.

Kingsland didn't go over anything twice. He was swift and he was thorough. Sunshine-roof, interior felt and foam, lights, hand-straps, mirrors, sun-visors, windows—each wound down and up—door pockets, seats, fascia, glove compartments, up under the dashboard, gear selector, seats, mats, carpet, ash-trays. Then the same top to bottom search in the back, the rear window shelf and stereo speakers included. It was all over in about a minute and a half, quicker than a wheel-change at Brands Hatch, it seemed; a professional display of the practised movements of one who normally had to do it to his own police car while a prisoner stood waiting—some inexperienced villain who had maybe thought the vital clue was safe down the back of Kingsland's seat.

D.C. Jones half-turned away. He thought so. Nothing. He reckoned he'd been pretty thorough. His neck muscles relaxed. A dented 1300 by the gate caught his eye; just like some family spaniel that'd been given a biting down the wrong street, he thought. Yes, the left-behind look of this place, the ownerlessness, made it just like a dog pound.

'Well, would you Adam-an'-Eve it?'

Jones tensed again as he turned to see Kingsland's backside protruding from the car like some suburban motorist busy with dustpan and brush.

'Look at this,' he said, 'stuck in a coil of the seat belt. . . .' Kingsland held up what he had found between thumb and forefinger, edge on, careful not to smudge any fingerprints on it.

'What is it, guv?'

'Well, you'd know better than me, Shakespeare; but I think I might just be able to manage this.' He squinted at it, turning it this way and that in the grey glare of the day.

D.C. Jones frowned and looked at it without touching. Oh, God, fancy missing this! 'Sorry guv.' There was nothing else to say; there was no excuse.

Kingsland didn't comment: no reproach, and no forgiveness. 'Well,' he said, 'a word with the car's real owner should clear up whether it's his or not; then with a bit of local leg work, Jonesey, even you should find the place it came from.'

Jones nodded again.

'Well, smile then. We could just wrap this up between us.'

Jones managed a sickly grin, like drinking his mother's home-made wine.

'And Jonesey....'

'Yes, guv?'

'Watch that Rover, it might bite....'

Smiling now, the case beginning to look cracked after a fruitless Sunday with the woman cashier from the stadium, Kingsland walked back to the station door holding the evidence carefully in front of him, while D.C. Jones followed obediently at his heels.

4

Like Ronnie, Manjit was no stranger to running home fast from school. She had further to go, but the first bit, near the school, was always the worst. Most of the Indian children in Clive Road went to the nearby Sandhurst Road School: but when Manjit's family had first come from Leicester there had been no room there, and the Education Office had sent her four blocks away to Ronnie's school. The High Street, separating Manjit's home neighbourhood from her school's, was as wide as the Indian Ocean, and her culture was as out of place around her school as a Jamaican's might have been around Clive Road. She had soon discovered that two streets in East London can be worlds apart, a discovery her parents and her elder brother had made before her, each in their turn; and she knew that to hang around after school was to be laughed at, or abused, or sometimes hit. Once a very kindly-looking old-age pensioner in a plastic rain hood and soft shoes had walked past her near the school, and had then turned and slapped her around the head. 'You know for why!' she'd hissed. So Manjit always ran; as far as the High Street, anyway; and she only began to feel relaxed when she got to the streets nearer home, where the turbans, the saris and the plastic flip-flops became more evident.

As usual, she was first in to the small terraced house. She shivered as the cold of the hallway hit her, and she made straight for the electric fire in the rear of the through-room. She put one bar on before going through into the small kitchen to plug in a kettle for some tea. She measured the exact amount of water to make three cups so that the kettle shouldn't boil needlessly, and she looked at the alarm clock by the sink to check that her timing was right. There was no room for waste in the Mirza household. Then she sat before the fire, rubbing her calf through her *salvar*, wondering whether or not to tell Sarinder, her brother, what had happened—and thinking about what her father would have said if she could have told him.

The whistle of the kettle and the next thud of the door coincided: and as Satya Kaur Mirza came in from the sweet factory Manjit ran to her and brought her into the living-room and sat her down. But there was certainly no telling her.

'The kettle's boiling,' she said in fast Punjabi. 'Sit down and I'll bring tea.' And before her mother could reply she had gone to be useful again in the kitchen; to bustle the place with life, and be grandmother and sister-in-law as well as daughter in the home. But it was only Sarinder, she knew, who could even begin to fill the family gap they all felt most keenly.

The atmosphere in Ronnie's first-floor flat was stale with cigarette smoke and old words. In the depressed stillness it was obvious that Steve and Val had long since exhausted talking about all the possible outcomes of the City East raid, and now all they had to do was sit about, or wander around stepping over the ash-trays and the empties of the emergency. Steve was still in his vest, his feet were damp in his socks, and he couldn't even lounge comfortably in the chair any more. Val had made herself up, but her mouth was set in a thin preoccupied line, the strain showed through like cracks in the make-up, and she didn't look up from pouring herself another Martini as Ronnie came in and dropped his swimming bundle on a chair.

Ronnie took it all in and went over to the television set. 'Wasson telly?'

Neither of them replied. Well, that was nothing new, so Ronnie shrugged and did what he usually did when there was a row on: he picked up a handful of sliced bread from the kitchen and walked back through the lobby into his own untidy room. He threw himself down on the bed and fumbled under it for his cassette recorder. He swore. It was going to be a long rotten night: best spent well out of their way. As if he didn't have enough worries of his own....

But he hadn't had time to turn the machine on before an urgent ring surprised the hallway, followed by a loud knocking, and suddenly the flat leapt into a frenzied life. Hell! Ronnie jumped up and stood tense behind his door, desperately going over what he'd been told to say, in case....

In the living-room the television was flashing on, and Val

was at the mirror, while Steve was scrambling into his shoes. It hadn't been Bradshaw's ring, or any of that lot, that was for sure. Steve tripped over a ruck in the rug as the bell went again, more impatient now, three times in a row.

'Come on, then,' hissed Val. ''Urry up, or they'll think you're stashing stuff under the floorboards....'

Steve looked at her, hard, and his stomach turned over. So there was no doubt in her mind, either. It was the law all right.

'You open the door,' he said. He tucked his shirt in and walked quietly on his toes out across the lobby into Ronnie's room. 'It's the police,' he told the boy, his eyes all over the room for some stupid mistake he might have made. 'I reckon.... Now, remember, don't say nothing till you're asked, and don't forget, when we went to football we *walked*, right? That's all. Other than that you 'aven't got to tell no lies. It's easy....'

Then Steve heard the click of the front door, and he suddenly felt very calm again. The wait was over at last and the contest was on. Now he was in a situation which his temperament understood.

He put his hands in his pockets and he walked casually out into the lobby.

'Yeah?' Val asked as she opened the door and stood back.

There were two men there; the first, a handy-looking fellow of about thirty in a blue quilted anorak who could easily have come from Bernie Bradshaw: but his partner, chewing, in a slim suit with a large knot to his tie, gave the game away. It was the law, definitely.

The man didn't take his hands out of his pockets, or bother to flash a warrant card: that was for the telly: they all knew what he was here for. He ignored Val.

'D.I. Kingsland,' he announced. 'You Stevie Webster?'

'Yeah. Why?'

'Well, we've done you, Stevie.' Already, he was looking beyond him. 'It's all over. You can put your hands up to this one, son.'

Kingsland and Jones stepped into the lobby, and Jones took the door from Val and shut it.

'If I knew what the 'ell you was on about it'd 'elp....' Steve didn't blink. If he could bluff his way into a bend at a hundred and fifty he could out-bluff this pathetic attempt.

'Oh, dear,' said Kingsland, meaning it. 'Come on, Stevie, I've got a lot on tonight....'

'Yeah, so've I, as it 'appens, so I don't want a lot of poncing around either. You'd better show me you ain't wasting my time....'

'No trouble,' said Kingsland, 'but do us a favour first, would you? Let's see your wrists, Stevie....' As he said it, Kingsland took Steve's hands and pulled them firmly towards him as if he were about to put the cuffs on.

'What you trying to do?' Steve watched Kingsland peering at the fronts, then the backs, before dropping them. 'You making sure I ain't been slashing myself?' He made a laughing noise.

'No, son, just looking for a drop of purple dye, a little tell-tale mark someone might have up under his rubber gloves. Didn't you know? One of the cashiers had a little go.'

'I wish I knew what the bloody hell you was talking about!'

'Yeah, of course you do. But then you were the outside man, weren't you? We've got something else on you, old son.' Kingsland jerked his head at D.C. Jones.

Jones was ready. The small brown envelope was already in his hand. 'Have a look at this, sir,' he said. And he showed the evidence to a frowning Steve.

Dutifully, Sarinder Singh arrived home from college at the expected time. Coming in and sharing the first cup of tea with his mother and his sister was important to them all because house-cleaning, cooking, and homework would pull them all in different directions until the three of them sat down to their evening meal together. He put his brief-case down in the passage and went through into the living-room. His mother was leaning forward on the settee, warming her hands before the narrow, metal fire, and staring.

He took her by the shoulders. '*Sat Sri Akaal*,' he said.

She patted his hand. '*Sat Sri Akaal*,' she replied. 'How are you? Sit down, there's some tea coming.'

It was a ritual exchange, but ritual was important: it preserved something of the old order of things.

Manjit brought in the cups and three digestive biscuits on a tray. Without a word she handed them round. There was a short silence, like at a funeral.

'What were you making today? Not Black Jacks again?'

Satya shook her head, and they both smiled sardonically. 'No,' she said. 'Penny Suckers today, with lemonade powder. But I'll please you both with some real sweets to-night, some *halwa* if you like. . . .' There was no time for them to nod, though, before she suddenly began to cry: not the wail of public sorrow, but the quiet tears of inner sadness. And then, as suddenly, it stopped, and she sipped her tea. It was often like that. Sudden, and over quickly.

'Your father always likes *halwa*,' she said.

So Sarinder and Manjit knew they'd have *halwa*, in his absence; and they'd leave his share on the plate, to be thrown out next day to the birds.

Steve Webster stared at the small rectangle of yellow card in D.C. Jones's hand. It was scruffy and dog-eared, the tacky clear-seal still grey with pocket grime. Steve's frown was genuine now, more squint and less furrow.

'What the 'ell is that?' he asked.

'Well you should know,' Kingsland said. 'You've got a son, haven't you? Ronald, Ronnie? Attends Elsmere Road School?'

'Yeah. So what?'

'And he's learning to read: gets extra lessons from a Miss . . .' he saw Jones's report in his mind's eye and read it there. 'From Miss Slessor, Lessor? Yes?'

'Could be. I don't know, do I? I don't know nothing about that school, 'cept they haven't done him much good. . . .' He looked at Val, but she was looking at the floor.

'Well, a little card like this was made at the school for the sole use of your son, by his teacher. For him to bring home and practise words with. See, it's home-made, felt-tip. . . .' He took the card from Jones and held it close to Steve's face, making him draw back. '"N . . . u . . . t—nut". In fact, because he lost one, the teacher's had to make him a new lot. And that lost one's been positively identified by the teacher; see, it's just like this: two little initials, in pencil. "R.W." . . . .'

'So?'

Kingsland stood balanced, his feet apart, his hands still in his pockets, but not relaxed there. Jones put the card back in its envelope and into his inside pocket, out of the way. The crunch was just about to come.

'So we found this card of your son's inside a stolen car, a car used for a get-away from the City East ground last Saturday, in which a man fitting your description—and a boy—were seen by six witnesses. . . .' Nobody moved. 'That's all. Open and shut. Bad luck, Stevie, it must've fell out of his pocket. . . .'

Steve looked at Val; and she looked back now, but she didn't blink, or smile.

'That's not evidence; that's circumstantial. . . .'

'Why, where were you and the boy Saturday afternoon?'

'Football, but that don't mean nothin'. . . .'

'Doesn't it? Wait till the identity parade. We've got enough. Stephen Webster, I'm arresting you for a robbery at City East Football Ground on the fifteenth of March last. You are not obliged to say anything unless you wish to do so, but what you say may be put into writing and given in evidence.' He said it fast, like a clever kid reciting a poem he'd had to learn.

'Nothing to say.'

'Right, get your coat.'

For the third time Steve looked across at Val; but she had turned her back completely and was walking back into the living-room. He flicked his leather jacket off a hook and slung it on a finger over his shoulder. He lifted his head up high to walk out of the front door of the flat.

And then he suddenly swung back away from the policemen, twisted round, and with all his force he kicked his right foot through the hardboard panelling of Ronnie's bedroom door.

There wasn't a word said that could be taken down: but then there didn't need to be.

Finally, clearing the twisted expression off his face with a great indrawn breath through his nostrils, he walked out of the flat.

And Ronnie, who had heard everything from a metre or two away, slumped back on his bed, first scowling, and then whimpering, like a kicked dog.

It must have been nearly half-past eleven that night when Manjit heard the cold tap of a car key on the window below her own at the front of the house. She'd heard it before, before her father had gone, and since; and now she was out of her bed in a matter of seconds to look at the large black car parked in front. It was very like the one the other night, she thought, the one the boy from school had been in; but now she could see where she'd been mistaken before; this car was longer, and it shone more in the light of the street lamp. The pavement was empty tonight though; and she went back to bed. There was nothing to be gained from being caught listening to them. They didn't want her to know anything or the man would have rung at the bell, or he'd have come earlier in the evening. Once before she'd had a sudden mad hope that it was her father downstairs, back for a secret night visit; but it hadn't been; how could it, when she knew only too well he was several thousand miles away?

'You'll have something to drink, sir?'

'No, son, I won't.'

Roy Bradshaw's hard nose twitched at the air, which was sweet with the smell of the *halwa*. He looked across at the Indian woman in the corner, wrapped up in her bright cotton and her hopes. As before, he ignored her and lit a panatella cigar, waving the smoke about like a joss-stick.

'Right, son, I'll tell you straight, then you can explain to your old lady in your own lingo. It turns out the dead man's passport didn't work. Your old man got stopped at Heathrow by the immigration people and got shot straight back to Delhi. Now that means he's down to pay for a return ticket, of course, so it's got to be some time before he can afford to have another go....' He said it brutally, with no thought for the boy's feelings, almost like putting the boot in.

'Yes, we know, sir. We heard about it from our friends who went to meet him....' Sarinder kept a straight face, swallowing the memory of their return from the airport.

'It's just bad luck, you see, son. It's no good your lot getting upset. No one's fault. Your old man was quite happy to take the money for letting us have his real passport, to get someone in. And it's no one's fault when the bloke gets caught with it. So it's hard, but it's a risk your old man ran. He understood that....'

Sarinder nodded. It had been for the best of reasons: a hundred pounds to help a relative out of financial troubles; but it had been stupid, truly stupid....

'Well, he had the choice. He could have paid the fine, or gone inside for a bit, and then it'd have been all over. But when he had to go back to India himself, well, we done the best we could, fixed him up with the dead man's passport, but it just didn't work. It turns out you lot don't all look alike to these immigration blokes after all....'

Sarinder looked at his hands. He said nothing. It was best. This man was still trying to help them, for a price.

'See, once he's back he can face the music and go on from there: they won't actually sling him out; not with you lot here. But he's got to *get* back, get past them barriers at Heathrow....'

'Yes.' Sarinder looked across at his mother. He knew she understood most of this. But she didn't interrupt by word or by gesture. It all sounded so hopeless—except this man hadn't come here tonight for nothing....

'Well, anyway, son, I was passing by and I thought I'd drop in and tell you that by chance I've got a little scheme going along other lines: we've had a setback or two, but certain ideas are being worked out, and later on I might be in a position to offer you a place, a sort of berth, so to speak—for your old man, if you want it.' He re-lit his dead cigar and stared across the tall gas flame at Sarinder. 'It won't come cheap. A lot of people are going to a lot of risk, you understand?'

'Yes....'

'But it stands a bloody good chance of working. Anyhow, that's about the strength of it at the moment. I just thought I'd sound you out. There's plenty want in, so there's no skin off my nose....'

'No. I understand, sir....'

'So anyway, write to your old man; make it 'ard for anyone else to follow what you're saying, you know; but sound him out on the idea of getting in by the back door; he'll understand. And we'll talk about money later, right?'

'Yes. Right, sir.'

'O.K., then.' Roy Bradshaw looked at his expensive gold watch, almost lost against a very broad leather strap on his wrist. He got up. 'An' tell the old woman it's traps shut all round. Or she won't see Daddy-o at all. Or Sonny Jim for that matter....'

Sarinder's stomach suddenly rolled as the man's meaning

hit him like strong drink: and all said so quietly, like friendly conversation.

'Yes, sir. Yes.'

'All right, then. I'll come back when you've had a chance to get a bit of news back. By then I'll have got a bit further on with my plans....'

'Yes. All right. Thank you, sir.'

'Good-night, then, love,' Roy called in a louder voice to Satya in the corner: and he went out to his big car.

Sarinder closed the door quietly and walked back into the living-room to find his mother on her feet.

'Open the window, Sarinder,' she said; 'please get that unclean smell out of the house....'

For a long time Ronnie hadn't heard anything but the faint sound of Val's radio. That evening, after the arrest, two other men had come back to ask him a few questions and search the flat, but only briefly, as if they weren't really expecting to discover anything. And then Ronnie had been left alone in his room to bury himself in a muddle of bed-clothes and shut out everything but the terrible feeling of responsibility for what had gone wrong.

What a stupid bloody thing he'd done! To Steve, of all people: the only one who sometimes had a bit of time for him. And now what? Well, that kick through the bedroom door said what: it said it all, didn't it? It said it was all over. His old man was sick of him, he couldn't trust him to do even a simple job without making a cock-up of it. He'd been warned about keeping his gloves on; and he'd helped with the lights in the car; so he'd known full well they were on a job. And then he'd been and given everything away by letting one of those stupid reading cards drop out of his pocket. Stupid woman, that cow Lessor, making him bring the cards home. Stupid bitch! Ronnie turned into his pillow and bit it, hard, until his head shook with angry effort. He punched the mattress. The cow! He hadn't asked for home-

49

work. He didn't want to read her stupid books. And now she'd made him do this. He'd got his old man nicked by the police, and that meant he'd put the finger on all the Bradshaws. Christ! What a mess!

Suddenly too hot, Ronnie turned and faced up to the ceiling, and thought about her. The smarmy, goody-goody, bitch, talking to the police. He could hear her voice, see her face, smell her stinking perfume. He bet she enjoyed that, telling them, dropping him in it. She hated him. She wouldn't have done it to that Paki. But him! 'Oh,' she'd say, 'what a stinking shame, Ronnie, but I had to tell them, you can see that....' The two-faced cow! Well that was her lot, because now all he wanted was to make sure he smashed her stupid face in before the Bradshaws came round and did him. A last act of revenge before they did what he knew they were going to do to him.

He spent a long time thinking how he'd do it. He clenched and unclenched his hands, his muscles tensed and twisted on the bed, and he tasted blood in his mouth as he drowned himself in the pleasure of thinking about doing something violent to Miss Lessor. Easy! It could be quick and painful, over in a couple of smashes, before that black girl could scream or run out for help. But it would last a lifetime, what he'd do. Then they could all do what they wanted. The teachers. The police. The Bradshaws. Because he wouldn't bloody care any more.

And then, somehow, with all the years of threats to himself finished with at last, and only the thought of something certain to come—because he'd let them down, and it *would* all happen now, like it had to Charlie Whitelaw—he felt better. Now it wasn't 'if' it happened, it was 'when': it could even be tonight: and Ronnie began to quieten, and to feel strangely settled. You could only be frightened by threats. Beyond threats, like in a fight, you began to exist on a strange level where somehow you weren't the one in it yourself. Whether the Bradshaws were going to do anything to

Ronnie Webster wasn't uncertain any more. And so now he didn't mind. But, God, if he got the chance, it was a great consolation to know he was going to do a few people himself on the way to his own destruction.

When he'd quietened, and his sweat was cold on the twisted sheets, Ronnie thought about Steve. He'd be in a cell somewhere, Shepherds Gate or East Ham, back in his socks and hating him. Lying there, wishing Ronnie had never been born. He groaned deep in his throat and looked again at the splintered door. It had been the only time they'd done anything together like that, him getting those lights out quick in the speeding car. He could still remember the funny feeling of pleasure he'd had inside: and now the way he'd spoiled it all made him want to run at the wall and just smash himself against it. Stupid idiot! He'd pulled his hanky out, or the stupid programme he couldn't read anyway, and he'd let that cow Lessor's stupid bit of stupid card fall out of his pocket....

He sighed, and lay there. He'd half expected Val to come in and swear at him; but she'd left him alone all evening so far. She must be as choked about what he'd done as his old man, Ronnie reckoned. She must be well pleased with him! He began to listen for her, to hear if she were throwing things about, or crying, or swearing; listening for the slam of the door to say she'd gone down the nick to see Steve. But as he strained his ears all he could hear was the radio in the kitchen. Listening to the news, seeing if Steve was going to be named, he guessed. Ronnie listened harder for some signal, anything to tell him her feelings; but as he listened he learned something else instead; he slowly began to realize that it wasn't the radio he could hear. Those tunes, in the order they were coming out, were on one of their own cassettes, weren't they? One of those Steve had recorded off 'Top Twenty'.

She'd got the stereo on.

Ronnie stood up off the bed and bent nearer the door.

Yes. It was their own stuff. No doubt. And not only that; not only that; she was singing! Not loud. But she was definitely singing.

He sat down again, shaking his head slowly with incomprehension. Like with books, he suddenly couldn't make sense of what was there before him: he couldn't read the situation. It was all too complicated, there weren't enough clues he could grasp and string together to make any sense. Not then.

It wasn't till the middle of the night, when the flat was quiet and dark, that he found himself back in that car with his dad for the thousandth time, leaning up to get that light off and not finding it easy: having to get right up off his seat because his jeans wouldn't give enough when he twisted. He remembered it clearly. And then he began to grasp at something so big he couldn't hold it in his mind all at once. Stiff jeans, they'd been; new jeans he'd worn specially for the match.

Christ! he thought as his throat suddenly closed, dry. The jeans he'd been wearing had never had a reading card near them in their life....

5

He didn't get it. It was diabolical, unbelievable. His already uncertain world had been first kicked, and then crushed, like a discarded beer can, and now Ronnie was so confused he couldn't plan putting on his socks properly, let alone carrying out the violence he'd promised Miss Lessor.

For days he muddled this way and that, went through some of the motions (like putting on his shoes) and forgot others (like doing them up). And he sniffed, and growled, and ran at strange sounds like a tame dog learning to be wild. Because the terrible thing was, now there was no one he could speak to in the world, not even his mother— perhaps *especially* not his mother. And that thought took some swallowing. God, he suddenly had a hell of a lot of sorting out to do.

He didn't waste his time going to school. He spent Tuesday wandering around the parks, and Wednesday walking along the raised scar of the sewer bank down towards the Thames. His pale eyes watered in the wind on the free ferry to Woolwich, and he was bumped and cursed as he ran back through the foot tunnel, not keeping to the left. He didn't eat much. As the week went on his pale skin became more transparent, and the freckles dark blemishes. He washed the front of his face, but that was all; and his hands turned grey, then black. He nicked an apple or a bar of chocolate when he wanted them; and he outran a policeman through East Ham market. But most of the time he walked, and thought.

After his father's brief court appearance on the Tuesday —remanded in custody pending further enquiries—there was only one thing to occupy his disoriented mind. The yellow card. That card in the car.

Why would his old lady have done it? She got fed up with him at times; hit him; pushed him off to bed: she definitely had her moods, and somehow the two of them just didn't have a lot to do with one another. But she gave him good grub as well; she bought him reasonable gear for best; she got him the cassette player; she sometimes poured him a light ale when they had a drink. So why should she have got one of those cards out of his old trousers and put it in his jeans? It couldn't have been to get shot of him, because he hadn't gone, he was still around. So why? Why should his mother have done it?

Or Steve? Why would his father? The threats of the Bradshaws had somehow made them feel in things together —a bit, anyway. Well, it made Ronnie feel close. And sometimes Steve would tell him about his racing days, and show him the old newspaper pictures and read him some of the cuttings. So why would Steve have done it? Besides, Ronnie thought bitterly, he wouldn't have put his boot into that door like that if he'd planned it all to get himself nicked, would he? Or would he? Ronnie tried to fathom it out from all angles. Perhaps if Steve had been threatened with a kicking—or worse—he might have got himself caught to be taken inside, to be safe. But no, Ronnie decided. You weren't safe from the Bradshaws inside. You weren't safe from them anywhere. And anyway, the card wasn't certain enough for that. To do that, all he'd have needed to do was leave his fingerprints on the wheel: or stall the car at the gate or pretend to bash into the traffic lights.

What about the Bradshaws then? Were they setting Steve up as an easy target for the police, letting him take the can back for the whole thing while they spent the money? Being clever about it, not making it too obvious? Steve wouldn't talk in prison, away from a bottle, they'd know that, wouldn't they? Ronnie went over that idea so many times in so many places. But wherever he was, this bit always came out the same. The Bradshaws didn't need anything like that to happen, because once they'd got away with the money Steve didn't come into it, one way or the other. Unless they were just doing him out of his share. And definitely, Ronnie told himself, that wasn't the Bradshaws. Besides, they'd had no chance to get near his rotten cards. Only Val and Steve had had that. Apart from Miss Lessor.

And the black girl had! God, yes! Too right! The idea of Manjit doing it came to him with the force of a sudden punch in the chest, when he was running through Wool-worths and he saw a kid like her, but who wasn't her; and he had to run out and down to the ferry away from people, wriggling through railings and dropping down to the stink-ing mud behind the pontoon to think.

She could have done it. Easy. Off the table and up her

sleeve, or something. They liked bright shiny things, those Pakis. Then she'd got chicken when she saw him that night and slid it in a crack of the window when the car was outside her house. Yeah! His eyes blazed and his mouth twisted. He threw a stone at a seagull but it fell a long way short. Yeah! That Paki. It could easy have been her. The more you thought about it the more it had to be right. There wasn't really anyone else it could have been, was there? Because how could it be his mum or his dad ... or one of his own people like the Bradshaws?

He rode the ferry for a bit, and somehow, that day, the ferry was smoother, the water clearer, less swirling dirt beneath the surface when he looked down into it. Yeah. That had to be the answer. He'd got to believe it. It was all too horrible to think of, otherwise.

Suddenly feeling better, he stole a ride on a 101 bus towards home and he said his first 'yes' and 'no' to Val again that evening. Now he badly wanted to say more, to bring it up with her; but she was still playing the stereo and singing softly—putting a bit of a brave face on things probably—and she dashed out and got him Chinese and a beer before she went out somewhere: but that evening, for the first time that week, Ronnie felt that he could at least sit down and watch the television without his stomach rolling over with the ache of uncertainty. He even shifted over to lounge in Steve's chair when the door had slammed on Val. And that night he went to sleep quicker than he had all week, feeling relieved enough to be able to save up thinking about the stupid black girl till the morning....

He told it with his eyes to the sprouting grass in North Woolwich Gardens. She needed stringing up for getting his dad put away—and for getting him the blame for it. He kicked at a daffodil, and it was her face: he stamped on a snail, and it was her head. Send them all back, all the stinking blacks: or line them all up against a bloody great big wall and stick bayonets in them. But he'd do something

55

to her Monday: like he'd been going to do to Lessor. He thought it all out, feeling good. For a long while his mind raced on the oil of violent invention. His day was a thousand atrocities. She'd never nick nothing of his again!

Meanwhile, the Bradshaws hadn't done *him*. He didn't know why they hadn't: except perhaps things never happened if you expected them to. When you were ready for anything nothing much ever seemed to happen at all.

That night he told Val about the girl, and she said she'd tell Steve when she saw him; and then he didn't see much of his mother all week-end; she did herself up and went out; and for two days she was more a mist of hair spray left in the air than a presence. But never mind. Ronnie had Monday to think about.

But Monday, when it came, wasn't like he'd seen it at all. After all the relish of anticipation, the drip of violence on his tongue, Monday was changed completely by what happened early on. It was after swimming again—or more like after bobbing up and down shivering in the shallow end, scared of the splashes and sullen at the instructor's scorn. It was on the coach, after sitting the unwelcome third in a double seat behind Charlie Whitelaw's broad back. They were all getting out, when the big driver had suddenly grabbed Ronnie's skinny muscle as he went past and said, 'You 'old on a minute, son.' Mr. Fleming frowned at Ronnie for doing whatever he'd done, touching the ash-tray or something, and left him to the driver's discipline. 'That's right, Mr. Whitelaw, you tell him. . . .' And when the coach had emptied Charlie had sat him down on the hot engine cowling.

'You're Stevie Webster's boy, ain't you?'

A long pause; deep scowl; thin tight mouth. 'Yeah.' Christ, was this it? Was this when he got done? Ronnie kept his eyes on the driver's hands as he rolled a cigarette. Well, it wouldn't be all that easy. No walk-over. He was ready....

'Stevie got nicked Monday?'

Ronnie just nodded. His mind was racing. From where

56

he was it was going to be hard to make the door behind him: but as soon as the big man took his eyes off him, even for a second, he was going.

'Shame, that.' Charlie Whitelaw lit his cigarette, and almost in a continuation of the same movement he flicked a switch beside him and the coach door hissed shut behind Ronnie.

The boy swung round, and then looked back again at the driver, his big, frightened eyes riveted on the stubbly face, his hands clenched white into the thin towel. He'd scratch his rotten eyes out if he tried to drive him off.

'Easy, son. I'm on your side, as it 'appens.... I just want a private talk, that's all.' And as if to calm Ronnie's fears Charlie Whitelaw switched off the vibrating engine and leant forward with his arms across the steering wheel in a non-aggressive attitude.

Ronnie kept eyeing him and took a fresh grip on his swimming bundle.

'Nasty shock, weren't it? Him going like that?'

Ronnie said nothing. No matter what the man said Ronnie wasn't going to commit himself about anything. With that scarred back to go on, the bloke could easily be putting on a friendly act, following Bernie Bradshaw's instructions.

'All a bit funny, and the least said, soonest mended, eh? But you listen, son.' Charlie turned in his seat to face the boy, eye to eye, and Ronnie suddenly found he couldn't take his eyes away even if he wanted to: because for the first time he saw the man's face, starting at his eyes, instead of just taking it in generally. And there he saw a younger man than he'd thought, with a sort of, well, different look to him: not so horrible: a bit more like someone's uncle than a Bradshaw villain who'd been taught to do as he was told. 'Now listen to me, Ronnie. . . .' The man's voice was quieter, and softer, than when he was shouting out orders on the coach; and he showed his teeth a bit in a sort of smile. 'Now listen. You've 'ad a bad turn; been done one an' all;

an' what I want you to know is, it's all *dirty*; you know; and it's worse than you think, son, I'm afraid. You'll know what I mean soon enough. But just remember....' and here he forced a stare out through his eyes, as if to impress Ronnie with what he was about to say. . . . 'when these dodgy goings-on come out, just remember I'm around, son. Right?'

Ronnie's mouth was open, and he felt dribble run down his chin. What the hell was all this....?

'Now, go on; clear off; I've said too much; and for God's sake don't you repeat it. But you just remember, right?' Then he flicked the switch to open the door and lit his cigarette again. 'Go on, off you get. Jump to it....'

And Ronnie did. Bewildered. Unsure. Unstable, like someone weightless in space. But as he went unsteadily towards the school, turning to see the coach drive off, all normal-looking, he saw Charlie Whitelaw's eyes before him: and while he still wouldn't trust him an inch, for the first time he found he wasn't picturing Charlie from the back; but from the front.

He was late again for *Poetry Time*, and Miss Neame shushed his entry and frowned silence at him while she mothered the transistor with her large bosom. Scruffy, miserable boys in trouble with the police shouldn't interrupt the poet's word, she seemed to say. But there wasn't a pamphlet for Ronnie to be bewildered by; and so he just slunk into his seat and let the others be bored by it. He had more important things to think about.

What the hell had Charlie Whitelaw meant? 'It's worse than you think'? Things couldn't get much worse than they were, could they? And what did he mean, *remember him*? It all beat Ronnie. But the man knew something was up, something wasn't right, didn't he? He knew there'd been something dodgy going on—he'd said it, hadn't he? Something dirty. Well, that threw one plan out the window: because where did that leave Manjit, the Paki girl now? There was definitely no way Charlie Whitelaw could know

58

about anything she'd done. . . .

Oh, God, he was all mixed up now—ten times worse than before! He thudded his knuckles into the desk, and the blunted anger of Ronnie's frustration, lacking direction, became an aggressive scowl around the room. Just let someone give him cause, that was all. Miss stinking Lessor could definitely look out in a minute: and whatever she'd done or hadn't done that rotten Paki girl had better keep well out of his way. . . .

When he'd kicked his way up the rises to Miss Lessor's room ten minutes later, Manjit, from another class, was already there; but when Ronnie bullied the door open the teaching stopped and everything was suddenly directed at him as if he'd walked into a surprise birthday celebration in his honour.

'Come on in, Ronnie, and sit down, love. . . .'

Miss Lessor's flat Manchester voice somehow made the syrup less sickening; but it still stopped him in the doorway, his feet apart and his hands clenched by his sides.

'Ere, what was all this, then?

'Come on.' Miss Lessor got up and went behind him to close the door. Then she gently propelled him to his usual chair with a small but firm hand in the middle of his back.

Ronnie allowed himself to go there with only a token resistance; but as he sat down he stared across the table at Manjit. What the hell was going on? What stinking scheme was this?

Manjit stared back for a second, awkward, mistrustful of his violence; and after only a second she looked down again at her book.

'I'm really very sorry, Ronnie, about this card business,' Miss Lessor said. 'I wanted to tell you all last week. I truly didn't know what they needed to know for, until after I'd told them. Although, of course, I should have had to, anyway. . . .'

There was a pause while Miss Lessor, still confident in

her sincere frontal approach to the delicate matter, half-closed her eyes to think of the best way of putting her next sentence.

'Oh, yeah?'

Ronnie was surprised that he'd spoken: he didn't know he'd decided to: and he certainly wasn't sure how he'd wanted it to sound.

'Oh, yes. The law's the law. But that's not to say I'm not very sorry about the way you were ... caught up ... in it, Ronnie. And not to say I'm not sorry about your father being taken away....'

Ronnie frowned. '*Not to say I'm not*'? What did that mean? Did that mean she *was* sorry? Or *not*?

'Now, I don't suppose you feel greatly like working with the new cards I've made you....'

Too bloody true he didn't!

'... So we'll do something else: try a new tack. We'll try linking your reading with some writing; and with real life, eh?' She smiled, her new mouth shining red, still very confident in her bold approach. 'I think you'll get something out of this....'

Trying to generate enough excitement for the two of them, she hummed a muted fanfare as she reached behind her into a cupboard and brought out a new exercise book. She opened it and creased back the cover. Ronnie's eyes, already lidded in rejection, saw that it was just an ordinary half-and-half book: the top half of the page blank and the lower half ruled in wide lines. Infant stuff.

'Now, you see, here we *illustrate*, do a picture....' Her long polished nails pointed to the white space. '... And underneath it we write a sentence or two about it; in our own natural words.'

Ronnie was frowning, and drawing back. It was still bloody work, wasn't it? Reading and writing.

'Look, here's Manjit's, to give you an idea.'

She twisted another exercise book round in front of

Ronnie, leaning forward over it to show him. The nails, and the hair-spray, and the make-up—and being all nice to him. It was a bit different to last Monday. Never the same twice, she wasn't—just like Val....

'See what Manjit's done?'

The first page in Manjit's book was very colourful. There was a picture of the head and shoulders of a man in a bright turban, smiling, with a beard; and in the background the sky was blue and there were very green, bushy trees. Underneath the picture there were two lines of writing; one in red biro, the other, underneath, in pencil.

'See, Manjit's written about her father; haven't you, Manjit?'

Ronnie looked at the words. But it was the same secret scribble it always was.

'Do you know what it says? Manjit, read it for us....'

Manjit didn't get up, but from where she was, upside down across the table, she read the words in a fast, high lilt.

'My dad's in India.'

'Yes, "My dad's in India." See, it's a book about her family. She's going to do a page about her mum, and about her brother, and so on.... All in her own words, so it's real ... real-life....'

Ronnie sniffed. Wasn't it marvellous the way people got worked up about rubbish like this? Real my backside! She wouldn't say that in a million years!

'Now, what about you? Manjit's book was closed and slid away, and the bare fact of Ronnie's first page was laid before him. 'Look, I've got you some felt-tips, Ronnie. We'll do the sentence together, then you can sit and do the picture till dinner time.'

The same old bribe again! Big deal! Do a picture! When the hell would they come up with something new? He'd been conned like this since the Infants. He sniffed. But the longest bits of the day did go quicker when you got on and did something; so he picked up his pencil like a chop-stick, and waited.

'Now, what can we write to make the book real, and exciting, and *yours*...?' Her eyes shone at him.

'Dunno.'

'Well think, Ronnie: you haven't thought.'

There was a long silence while Ronnie waited to be told. They always told you in the end.

'Well, what about like Manjit? It's sad, we know, but it's a fact; it's true, isn't it? It'd make a real book if you wrote something about *your* dad....'

Like what? Like 'My dad hates me because I got him nicked'? Would that bloody do her? He scowled, but he waited. She'd start writing something in a minute; then he could copy it underneath.

'Well, what about a short sentence like, "My dad's gone away"?' She looked at him without blinking, and her smooth white hand briefly patted the grime on the back of his. 'Eh?'

He sniffed.

'You see, being real, it might be more help than cards, and books; you can see how reading is part of life....'

He shrugged. At least it wasn't too long to copy. And who cared what the rotten words said? They were *nothing*. But he definitely wasn't going to sit and draw her a picture of *his* dad. Doing what? Kicking his door in? He didn't want to even think about all that till he'd had a chance to sort it out with him.

Or in the car at the football?

He suddenly stiffened. God, was this a take-on to get a bit more evidence for the old bill?

'There we are, then.'

The words were on the page. Miss Lessor looked at them with pleasure and drew in a long, satisfied, breath.

Setting his mouth as if the book were a bottle of medicine, Ronnie began copying the red words on the wide line below. But he had hardly begun when a slight snuffle made him look up. It was the girl. She was working on her own half-and-half book, and she was crying.

'What's the matter, Manjit, love? Don't you feel well?'

Manjit shook her head.

'Tummy-ache? Or head-ache?'

Manjit looked at Miss Lessor through her tears. You don't understand, her misery said; and even Ronnie could read that much on her face. But Manjit just sniffed and shook her head. 'No miss,' she said.

Then Ronnie broke his pencil, and swore quietly. Stupid bloody idea, this was....

6

Detective Inspector Johnnie Kingsland sat back in The Rose and drank the half of lager he'd allowed D.C. Jones to buy him.

'Not a bad boozer, this,' he said. 'Better since it changed hands....'

'Yes, so they say, guv. Decent atmosphere for a lunch time....'

'I mean more villains use it since the old boy died.'

'Oh. Yes.' Business, always business, the guv'nor: no time for anything else.

'I stayed in here one night, over in that corner, after time was called. Half the villains in London was in here: both the Bradshaws, all their hangers-on: all drinking till the early hours. This is where to come to get your card marked, Jonesey, when one of them wants to put another one away....'

'Oh....' Jones looked round the bar and tried to see them

all with the guv'nor's eyes. Not just a bar full of thirsty drinkers, but a lounge of leisured young men, well turned-out in their expensive shirts, or leather jackets, or suede 'bombers'; the shoes with gilt toe-caps; and hardly a woman in sight. All there for a purpose. 'Stevie Webster, guv? Reckon someone here might tell us a bit more than he will himself?'

'Well, I had hoped. But I've shown myself, and no one wants to know me, so I reckon we've drawn a blank.' He downed his beer and shook his head when Jones indicated getting another. 'No, we'll push off. But we haven't wasted our time. At least it confirms what we're thinking. The football job must've been the Bradshaws' little work of art; because it's funny otherwise that no one in here's talking about the grab of the year. They're not talking about anything else in the other pubs around. But not in Bradshaws' boozer. Not when we're around. With any other mob we'd have had half a dozen trying to settle old scores off us.' Jones sipped at his pint and put the glass down gently. 'No, you can often tell as much from what doesn't happen as what does. . . .'

D.C. Jones nodded. He was smart, Kingsland: and single-minded. He'd only come in for a drink, himself! But as he set about swigging it back quickly he suddenly saw something which started him coughing and spitting into his glass.

'God, Jonesey, I just wanted to show myself, not put on a bloody pantomime. . . .' But when he saw what Jones had seen he swiftly turned his own head away.

It was Val Webster, just come in, quietly and smartly dressed; made-up; hair in a new bubbly style; looking good. She was too tense to look about her, so she didn't see the policemen: but they saw her, being welcomed deferentially at the bar by one or two young men, with no liberties being taken, and a drink called for immediately by someone who knew what she had.

'Of course, she could have just come in for Stevie's share,' said Kingsland; 'but I don't reckon. We could hang around to see who she's with, but we won't push our luck. Though it wouldn't need more than two guesses out of three to know who'll be in in a minute....'

Jones composed himself, eyes watering. 'Yes, O.K. Sorry. It went down the wrong hole,' he muttered.

'Too right, Jonesey. Just like that little vixen over there.' Kingsland stood up. 'Come on, Shakespeare, I've got an idea where I might show up this afternoon....'

Anyone watching might have been suspicious, if they hadn't been too preoccupied with their own problems. There was the car, a run-of-the-mill Ford, neither old nor new, and there was the man sitting in it, watching the children come out of school. And from the way he was watching and waiting it was clear that he wasn't a father on a regular pick-up: the man was staring too intently at the children for that, as if he were frightened of missing the one he wanted.

From the car, parked just off the zigzags, he had a good view of the school gate and of the children coming out; and at 3·45 he saw the first cluster, a mixed group of bigger boys, grey London white and brown London black, still energetic at the end of the day in spite of the balls and bags of swimming gear they were carrying; pushing and jumping, and neatly tripping with violin cases between the ankles. Then some younger ones, boys and girls; an Indian girl in a turquoise *salvar-kamiz*, running fast: and then, pinched and shivering slightly in the April breeze, a scruffy boy in a thin shirt, grubby flares and old trainers: walking slowly as if he'd nowhere special to hurry towards. He walked past the car and the man leaned over and wound down the near-side window.

'Ronnie? Ronnie Webster?'

Ronnie's scared suspicion flashed in his eyes. One of Bradshaw's? His toes curled ready to run. But he'd heard the voice before, hadn't he? Not all that long before....

'I'm Detective Inspector Kingsland. From the police. I came round to your flat last Monday.'

Yeah. Sure. He knew he knew that voice. When would he forget the sound of the talking that night?

'Well, you look a bit like your school photograph. The same serious face. Here you are, jump in; I want a quiet word.'

They all did, didn't they? Charlie Whitelaw, now this bloke. But Ronnie got in, without any fuss. He knew who the bloke was. He knew he definitely wasn't from the Bradshaws. So what did he want? Was he putting him away, too? He didn't care if he was. All ways up, it didn't make much odds.

Ronnie kept his eyes down and stared at the empty glove shelf as the car moved off.

'It's all right, Ronnie, you're not in any trouble. . . .'

Christ, he was joking!

'This is unofficial. I'm not asking you any questions, or anything. I'm not allowed to, anyway, not without someone's permission. No, I was just passing, and I saw the others coming out; and I thought if I saw you I'd tell you how your dad is.'

It was all very smooth.

'I don't suppose your mum's had a lot of time to get over and see him with you and the place and everything to look after?'

'Nah.' It came from deep in Ronnie's throat. What was that to him? All right, it had struck *him* as strange that she hadn't, but what was this berk on about it for?

'And she works as well, doesn't she? Not much spare time?'

Ronnie shook his head, just a bit. 'Nah.'

'I must've got it wrong, then. Anyway, Ronnie, your dad's not too bad, as it happens. He's on remand, that means although he's in Brixton he's not a convicted prisoner. Not yet. He's treated different, you know. Only we've got to hold him there for a bit while we carry on with our enquiries.' There was a long pause while Kingsland overtook a shivering milk float. 'Only we all know he's taking the can back for someone else. . . .'

In the silence Ronnie sniffed. He wasn't saying nothing to that. What did the bloke think he was, stupid?

'Yeah, it's only a question of time before we tie the ends up. Then your dad can get convicted for his small part of it, and he can start getting his sentence done. And the sooner he does that, the sooner he gets home. . . .'

Still silence. Huh! The sooner you do the sentence the sooner you can do the nice picture! They were all the same, kidding you on, whatever sort of sentence they were talking about!

'Anyway, he's all right. Now, when I see him—this is what I wanted to say—when I see him in the morning, can I give him a message from you?'

The car moved on in its line of traffic and took a couple of turnings; but Ronnie said nothing.

'No? No message?'

Another turning.

'No?'

'Nah.'

'Just give him your . . . love, eh?'

Ronnie sniffed again, and then after half a street he nodded.

'O.K. Now, which is your block?'

'Kingston.'

'Oh, yes.' Kingsland drove along the narrow road, reading the names let into the yellow bricks. Richmond House, Twickenham House, Windsor House. No, not this one.' He squinted out at the official names, decorated with curls of aerosol spray. 'They all look alike to me. How do you know yours, Ronnie? Do you count them?'

Ronnie shot a look at the policeman: defensive at first, then knowing. Christ, the man was sharp. He'd heard about the reading, and he was checking on those stupid cards being his; checking he'd needed them! That meant he was even checking on what Lessor must've told him. Ronnie sniffed, and looked at the line of identical towers. Well, clever copper, he knew because he lived there, that's how. How did a fox know his own den? Little things. A broken window, a spray pattern on the wall, the oil where a particular car stood. Just the feel of the place. But not only that, as it happened.

'I read it, don't I? On the wall. Kingston.' There was defiant pride in the way he said it.

'Oh, that's great.'

Pick the bones out of that, copper! But it was true, anyhow. He saw 'Kingston' often enough to know it, for Crissake.

'Well, O.K., Ronnie. Here you are. "Kingston" it is.' The detective leaned across and opened the door for him. 'I'll give your dad that message for you,' he said quietly. And then in a very matter-of-fact voice he added, 'I used to have a bit bother with words myself. Still do, spelling. . . .'

Ronnie slammed the door and the man went. He swore, obscenely, and spat three or four times, head back, high and defiantly after him. I've seen through you, mate! it said. So don't come your smarmy stuff with me. . . .

It was getting on for eight o'clock before Ronnie began seriously listening for Val. They'd never been a regular family, with meals at definite times, coming and going in a way you could set your watch by. They did things as they pleased; and when they all happened to be in together she got something to eat—or sent Ronnie out for it. So it wasn't until he began to feel hungry that he started wondering where she was. He ate some slices of bread and drank some milk from the bottle, and he watched some more television. Then he turned the set down a bit and listened to people's voices around him, lift doors opening and closing on other landings up the shaft, and he waited for the slow slide of her key in the lock.

Perhaps she'd gone to where that copper said, to see his dad....

That copper: Kingsland. And Charlie Whitelaw. And old mother Lessor. Christ, he'd been spun about today by the lot of them, like some kid wearing a blindfold at a stupid party. The trouble was, trying to think out all they'd said was like listening to the stereo, or putting something on the cassette; the more sounds there were going in, the quicker it all became just a loud mess of noise and you couldn't make any sense of it.

The last clear thing he could go back to was blaming that girl for the card in the car. Then, because Charlie Whitelaw knew about it all, he'd got confused. Now, the copper had checked up on Lessor, so *she* could be dodgy. But then the berk didn't know Val didn't go out to work, so perhaps he knew nothing after all. Ronnie screwed his face up with the frustration of being confused. And how about Kingsland trying to come all matey at the end, saying about him being a bad speller. Trying it on, wasn't he? Which made two today, because Charlie Whitelaw had gone on about how he was on his side—God, they all did it! So where did that leave the card business! Christ, it was all like a loud shout in his ear!

Well, one thing was sure as hell. He definitely hadn't taken the card with him in that car. He'd been in the wrong jeans. So.... Oh, God, he was all mixed up again....

Now where was she? He was hungry for more than stinking dry bread.

Ronnie watched the television for another quarter of an hour, until a commercial for Colonel Sanders take-away chicken finally stirred him out of his chair. Perhaps she'd left money for chips on the mantelpiece? She did that sometimes when she was going to be late.

He ran his hand swiftly along the tiles like an experienced thief. No, nothing there but a folded-over brown envelope. Some old bill they hadn't paid. He slouched back to Steve's chair, and then it suddenly struck him that she might have left some money in the envelope. If she'd paid someone at the door....

Thank Christ. She had. Fifty pence! Enough for chips and something else. But hold on! There was a note with it. Probably told him what to get with it. He opened it. Oh, stuff that! He'd get what he wanted. Pie and chips, open, to eat walking back. And a can of Pepsi....

With the faintest glint of pleasure Ronnie put the note and the money in his trouser pocket and went for the door. At least he could have one of the things he wanted.

When he woke up in the chair the light was still on and the television was humming blindly. He looked at the clock. It was two o'clock: or ten past twelve: he was too tired to focus his eyes and sort it out. He got out of the chair, pressed the set off, and wandered towards his bedroom. She might have woken him up when she came in, he thought. Probably had a few too many with one of her mates and gone straight to bed without thinking. That was nothing new. He threw himself down on his own heap of bedclothes, pulled something over him, and carried on sleeping; too tired, even, to dream.

The light in his room was flat and bright when he woke again, and the sounds around were unfamiliar for normal getting-up time: no cars in a crawl, but women talking outside the flats; small kids crashing tricycles, a half-empty milkman shouting out something rude.

Was it Saturday? Couldn't be. There was more noise than this, Saturday. He sat up and shivered. He was still in his clothes! He frowned. Once more the signs didn't make any sense. He opened the splintered door. There was the *Sun* on the carpet. No, he knew it wasn't Sunday. But now he remembered: last night; Val being late.

Wasn't she up yet? She must've had a skinful, and let him sleep on. Well, she couldn't have a go at him for being at home if she didn't get him up for school.

Ronnie went to the bathroom. The room looked lighter, barer, as if the curtains had been taken down: but they hadn't. It must be the time, Ronnie thought: after all, it was later and lighter than when he went to school.

He walked through the darkened living-room; but he didn't stop to open the curtains because he'd just thought of a quick way of doing her a favour. A cup of tea and two Alka-Seltzer's: that's what Steve always got. He made two mugs and took one through to Val in the big bedroom, spilling some as he picked up the paper on the way. But she'd say thanks for that; reading her stars in bed.

Carefully, he opened the bedroom door. The daylight from the big window made him blink. The *Sun* slipped and tea slopped as he craned his neck further round the door. Bright daylight. Curtains open. Bed-cover on. Fitted cupboards open, half empty.

Eh?

No Val.

'You there?'

But he knew she wasn't. She hadn't come back last night. Had she been arrested too?

He put the mugs down and banged through a search of the flat. Hell! There were coats gone, some dresses, shoes, make-up; bathroom sill empty of lacquers and talcs. You didn't take that lot to prison: more like holiday packing, that was. He banged round again, like a frightened sheep in a pen. She'd gone all right. But why? And where?

At last he sat down, and sniffed. Bloody funny, this was. But she'd ring up in a bit. Tell him where she was; where he had to go to meet her. She'd gone into hiding, hadn't she?

Yeah. That was about it.

71

So he'd have a wash, put on his new jeans, and be ready. Because this had to be some sort of plan the Bradshaws had set up; or something Val and Steve had worked out on their own; some dodge to get the two of them out of the way of creeps like Kingsland.

Ronnie took off his trousers and turned out his pockets for change. There wasn't much, just a few pence, and the brown envelope it had been in. And the note. The note! Stupid berk, he was! Yeah, she'd written him a note, hadn't she? Standing there, in his underpants, he unfolded it and blinked.

But it was no use. However important it was, it was still just a jumble of scribbles that told him nothing. He stared hard at the paper, frustrated, focusing and refocusing, as if it were his eyesight at fault: but it was no good. What lay between 'Dear Ronnie' at the top and 'Mum' at the bottom was a foreign language to him.

Oh, hell! So was she coming back today, or not? Was she going to give him a ring? Or did she want him to go off somewhere and meet her? Was the fifty pence a bus fare, or for a taxi? Or was he supposed to go and get a bit of dinner in?

Stupid bitch! She could have known he'd have a bit of trouble with a note. *So what was supposed to happen?*

Ronnie got dressed slowly and didn't bother with the wash. Well, she'd ring when he didn't do whatever it was he was supposed to. He went into the living-room and sat in Steve's chair again, sniffing and blinking and watching a baby programme, and then the school broadcasts. But the telephone didn't ring. Eventually it was the chill in the flat that sent him back into his bedroom for his leather top, for a second accidental look at the note on his bed: and then it clicked. What he'd been watching, some rubbish about reading, had put Manjit into his head; and now, seeing the note again.... He ran back into the living-room to look at the clock. Just time for it, if he hurried. He made sure the television was off, he checked the key-string round his neck, and out he went, stuffing the note into his pocket as he ran.

He got on to the end of the school dinner queue without any bother. They were always a few plates short, or a few plates over. The meal that day was fried egg and mash, and rice pudding: and Ronnie was lucky, because Manjit could eat that, and she was sitting in the far corner of the canteen. There was also an empty space next to her.

He saw her look up when he went over. First she smiled, then she frowned, bewildered: and he blew his chest out slightly when he realized she was wondering whether he was going to hurt her today. He slid down beside her quickly, before she could get out.

''S all right,' he said. 'I ain't gonna 'urt you.' He sniffed, and said slowly, 'Me no 'urt.... 'Old on a minute.' He forked into his dinner with his head lowered, his eyes on his plate at first, and then, as he slowed, he took in the canteen. The tables were emptying, and there was no one much near.

''Ere,' he said, reaching into his pocket for the note. 'Read us that.' There was no hesitation with him now he'd eaten. He knew what he'd decided to do, and he was doing it. From the blank look on her face he felt sure he'd made a good choice, too; she wouldn't go round the school shouting about having to read his note for him, not like any of the English would. This was more like trusting the cat. Anyway, he told himself, there wasn't no one else, was there? And he had to know where Val wanted him to go, and what to do.

Without the confidence to sit and read the note through first, Manjit started on it as soon as she had unfolded it. She clearly had no idea what it might be. It could have come from Miss Lessor—her only link with the boy—or Miss Lessor might possibly have made him write to say he was sorry for hitting and kicking her.

'"Dear Ronnie,"' she began. No, it was the boy's all right, not hers. '"Sorry but I won't be home...."' She read

73

in her new reading voice, still accenting the words and stressing the sentences with Punjabi rhythms. But the message came through clear enough; clear, and cold enough to freeze the inside. ' "Tell your dad I've gone off for a bit. I left 50p for your dinner. I haven't got no more change. Tell them down the school and you'll get put in care. It's all right, I was, you'll be O.K. Be seeing you. Your loving Mum." '

Ronnie spooned up the rice pudding until he couldn't pretend there was any more to spoon, and he let the spoon lie. He concentrated on the plate, the rim chip, the blemished surface, until he knew that plate like his bedroom ceiling. He sniffed a few times, but he didn't say anything. Neither did Manjit. They just sat, the boy bewildered and bereaved, and the girl hemmed in by it. The canteen had emptied, the service shutters were down, and the banging of the pots was muted. A lifetime away a whistle blew, and the noise Ronnie hadn't heard, the yell of children playing, slowly subsided.

Then suddenly he snatched the note, and he scraped back his chair, and he ran.

7

While they drank their tea together that afternoon Manjit told her mother and Sarinder about the boy and the note. It was a big thing to have been so close to, like seeing a building fall down: but her shock wouldn't wash off as easily as brick dust would. Even so, the force of her mother's response took her by surprise. Satya Kaur shook her head and made a loud clicking sound of disapproval with her tongue.

'These English people certainly have some strange ways of carrying on,' she said. 'In Jullundur your father's family would have seen to it that I was never welcomed by decent people again.' She clicked her tongue once more. 'It is unthinkable. Only a father will leave his family: and then only for a proper reason, like seeking work, or coming to England to get a better life for the family. . . .'

Sarinder nodded, but Manjit frowned. Then what of her father? she suddenly wanted to ask, now that the longed-for opportunity was here at last. What was his proper reason? He would have one, she knew; her honoured and loving father; but what was it? Why was there so much mystery about him? He hadn't gone away to work, when he'd gone away from them. So why had he gone? Her frown deepened, but she said nothing. Her mother rarely talked about her father these days; and she knew her questions would be unwelcome. There must be reasons why she hadn't been told. The boy's situation suddenly seemed to have brought them back to the familiar territory of their own loss and their own silences. A deep sadness grasped at her, an acute pain among the dull ache: and she couldn't help but envy slightly the boy who at least had had a note.

Ronnie had run back to the flat. There was nowhere else to go. The parks and the sewer-bank were all right for someone on the run; but there was only one place for someone who wanted just a private hole to crawl into: and that was home.

He saw nobody as he ran, neither the pedestrians he pushed aside nor the motorists he pulled up. He ran along pavements and across roads, his eyes hardly leaving the ground, and when he got to Kingston House he unlocked the door, ran into the living-room, and threw himself full-length on the settee.

The cow! All right, so she swore at him more often than she smiled, and she was a greedy bitch, all out for herself:

but to clear off now, when his dad couldn't have it out with her: that was filthy! He lay there on the firm settee, eyes dry and his body bony and comfortless in its misery. He just couldn't cry. Somehow crying was the last thing he wanted to do. But he badly wanted to kick something, or to smash it in. Badly. He thumped up dust with his fists, and he swore. And the rotten way she'd done it! Letting him let that Paki girl know! She could've rung him: but writing him a note! That just about said it all about how much she bloody cared! He knuckled his dry eyes, and sniffed. Well, he wasn't going to tell anyone. He'd be all right here for a bit. No one had to know, did they?

And then it suddenly hit him. Why the hell should he be on his own? He didn't have to be. Not for long. No. They'd let Steve out. They'd have to, because *he'd see to it*. This changed everything. Now he could do it. And one word from him would be enough, wouldn't it?

He sat up and tried to seriously figure it out. They were only hanging on to Steve to get the Bradshaws. That was clear as daylight; well, that copper had said it, as good as. And, of course, Steve would never let that happen. But if *he* fingered them, Ronnie, then they wouldn't need Steve, and they could let him out on bail. And he could do it, too, because he'd heard some of the talking, heard the threat, seen them going down the pub, been in it at the football. There was a hell of a lot he knew. Yes, if *he* did it he'd get Steve out like a shot....

And then? The cold thought of angry Bradshaws sent a warning down the skin on his back: the tingling fear that they had always counted on to keep his mouth shut tight. If they got to him first, he thought. Well, perhaps him and his dad could do a bunk out of it altogether. Abroad. Well, out of it somewhere. Somewhere so's they wouldn't end up being dug up side by side from some farm down Essex....

It was possible, wasn't it? There were places they could run to, out of reach? Yeah. There must be. The only real

76

problem, now he'd decided, was how to get word to the copper. How to do it without being sussed by the Bradshaws. This would all take a bit of thinking about.

Ronnie stood up. But what now—till he'd got it all worked out? He looked round the room, and he thought on his fingers. Well, he had to make sure he could get by in the flat for a bit. Electricity was all right. They were all electric in Kingston House, paid it with the rent, he thought. So he'd have a light and he could watch telly if he got scared or lonely. That was O.K. He went into the small kitchen. But grub was the aggravation. Val never kept much in, and there was only a packet of tea and a couple of cans of he-didn't-know-what in the food cupboard. He recognized the blue label of the baked beans, and there was a bit of cheese in the fridge, and half a pint of milk; but he wasn't sure about anything else. Anyway, he was all right for tonight: and the milk would keep coming for a bit. No, he could hold out for a while—do a bit of nicking if need be—just as long as no busybody in the flats went reporting he was on his own to the council.

But now—he wandered back into the living-room, *his* living-room, and stood by the big window—how was he going to tell Kingsland? He pushed his nose hard against the net curtain, a stocking-mask face looking out. Well, he wasn't walking up to the counter at the nick and asking to see him! It was going to need to be a bit more clever than that. And he wouldn't be writing him no notes, neither! He sucked air through his teeth with a whistle, and scowled. Well, that only left hanging around outside the nick some-where, hoping to see him going in or coming out: that was a bit more like it: if he kept himself out of sight, in doorways. No! Hold on! Ronnie spun round, leaving the nets in a muddle. Yeah! No sweat! He'd got the phone, hadn't he? And that 999 was easy enough. It always looked dead simple on *Police Five*.

He looked at the ivory instrument, a dead end, sitting

there waiting for someone to do something with it. Well, how about it? Should he pick it up and get things going now; or let things ride for a bit and see how it all worked itself out tomorrow? Yeah, he'd do that. It wasn't urgent for the minute, because there was no way anyone was going to get him put in care. No, a day wouldn't matter. But now was a good time to get the things ready, anyhow; the evidence. Ronnie suddenly shivered and switched on the log fire, then he bolted the front door and went into his bedroom to get what he wanted, the printed card to prove they'd been to the football, and the brand-new red and white bobble-hat with the price sticker still inside it, just to show it was never a regular thing. They'd help. But best of all there was his word: and by Christ he knew enough to make that count....

The sudden shrill of the doorbell almost made him yell out with surprise and cold fear. God, who was this? No one he knew rang like that. His chest thumped while he tried to think. It could be the milkman, for his money, or it could even be Bernie Bradshaw: and the stupid thing was that one was as bad as the other, at that moment. He couldn't afford to see either of them. If he wasn't really clever the milkman could give him away and send him off on the run, to live wild and sleep rough. While Bernie Bradshaw could just break his legs and stop him running altogether! He froze, and felt the blood pounding in his head. It could have been a lot of people: a hell of a lot: but it wasn't Steve, and it wasn't Val; they had keys: and it didn't sound like the ring and the rap of the law. So who was it? Well, one thing was certain, Ronnie's instincts told him; it wasn't likely to be anyone who could do him any good.

He decided not to answer the ring. Hold tight and they'd clear off, he told himself. It was probably going to be a lot like this from now on. He was going to have to lie low and be deaf. He stood still in his bedroom and stared at the front door, holding his breath. And he only just stopped himself from arching erect and screaming loud as his spine, a shiver before his brain, suddenly told him that something was staring at him through the letter-box: a man, the eyes low down and out of place, like a hand coming under the door. Ronnie's body was paralysed; and he knew sudden terror, a multiplication of fear.

'Come on, Ronnie,' said a voice strained in a stoop, 'let me in....'

It was Kingsland.

'Come on, I'm on my own this time....'

Kingsland! The shock was over already, leaving him cold and numb. But now the frantic worry. It was on a plate, he didn't even have to lift the phone. But could he? Would he tell him?

No. Not now, anyway. The thought of it being Bradshaw had made him realize he wasn't ready yet. He couldn't be sure he'd thought out all the angles, and he had to be sure. Oh, God! Ronnie knew that he had to be jumps further ahead in his thinking before he opened that door. As his heart thumped his brain tried rapidly to make some plans.

He had to have time to think everything out, right? So, lose the evidence for the time being and think later. He threw the card and the hat behind him into his bedroom and shut the door. Stall him. Let the bloke in and pretend his mum was only down the shops. Get rid of him, then think out what to do....

'Come on....'

Ronnie reached up to let him in.

'Hello, bolted yourselves in?'

They didn't miss a trick, these.

'No school today, then?'

Up yours an' all!

'I came to see your mum....'

The eyes at the front door went everywhere at once and Ronnie knew inside, suddenly, but definitely now, that there was no way he could trust this man. You could tell, he thought. Like with teachers, you'd know which coppers you could trust when you found any. And he hadn't yet. Whatever they were up against, him and Steve, there was nothing the same between them and this bloke. They were just on different bloody sides. And that's where they'd always be.

'Is she in?'

Ronnie shook his head. 'Down the shops.'

'Oh, well I'll wait, if you don't mind, Ronnie.'

Ronnie stared him straight in the eyes, and shrugged. Kingsland walked through into the living-room, and, moving a crumb-covered plate, sat in Steve's chair. Still Ronnie could see him taking everything in, the crumpled curtains, the rucked rugs, the dusty fire still pinging as the metal expanded: all the signs of a neglected room recently re-entered. Ronnie didn't know what to do: sit down, stand up, clear off.

'Reckon she'll be long?'

'Dunno.' Ronnie was tempted to say more, make up a story about her going on out somewhere from the shops; but some instinct told him not to overplay it; to be patient and see it through bit by bit.

'Bunked off from school, have you?'

'Yeah.' Ronnie shrugged. He was playing it really clever now, letting the man believe he'd committed some small crime, so long as it wasn't the big truth.

'What did your mum say?'

'Didn't mind.'

'Had your dinner?'

'Yeah!'

Well, he had, although not here in the flat with Val. But they both knew that answer had been too quick. The policeman sat back in the chair.

'You're on your own, aren't you, Ron? She's gone, that's about it, isn't it?'

Ronnie scowled. 'No! 'Course she ain't!'

'Oh, come off it, Ron. You know I've only got to go and

look in her bedroom.... '

Panic shattered Ronnie's defensive mask. God, no. He couldn't let him look round the place. He'd be thorough. He'd see the special football ticket and everything. . . .

'Only from last night. She's coming back.... '

Kingsland looked hard at Ronnie, like a teacher telling him to think again. Then his eyes lost the sharpness of their focus, and he tut-tutted slowly. 'It's a rough old turn-out, Ron,' he said, and he got up and walked through into the kitchen. 'Not much food, is there?' He looked about, turned things round, checked for food in places where Ronnie knew it was pointless looking. 'No, not a lot. . . .' he said to himself. He picked up a cheap ball-point from a groove in the draining board. 'Left you a note, did she?'

Ronnie shook his head; but his right hand involuntarily jerked a few centimetres towards his trouser pocket, and Kingsland's eyes had spotted it. He shrugged again and dug down for the note, handing it to the policeman.

Kingsland read it and he shook his head. 'She's not much better than me,' he said as he folded the paper and handed it back. 'Rotten speller.' He went over to the living-room window, straightened the net, and looked out, his arms folded across his chest; and he stayed like that for what seemed like five minutes, occasionally drawing in his breath noisily and letting it out on a long whistling sigh: the sounds of difficult decisions. Ronnie could have run then. But they both knew that he wouldn't. Not when he thought about it; not with the possibility of D.C. Jones standing outside the front door.

'So you need your old man out, Ronnie,' Kingsland said at last. 'Don't you?'

But Ronnie didn't respond. He just stood leaning against the wall by the door, as straight and unrelaxed as a plank, and he watched Kingsland as he walked back into the kitchen once more and heard him bang the fridge door. The man came back, zipping his coat.

81

'I get off about six,' he said. 'I'll bring in some cod and chips: you like that, don't you?'

Ronnie frowned.

'Oh, you're all right here by me, Ron. I've got no cause to shift you: not till we've sorted something out that'll suit us both. So don't go spoiling your appetite with any beans or anything. I'll see you later.' He didn't wait for a reply: but walked out of the flat and along the corridor to the stairs with his head up and his eyes sharp; looking like a man who was on the edge of something.

Ronnie's instincts told him that he'd probably got time to rake together one or two bits before he went. And he'd got to go, he knew that, if only because that cocky copper thought he wouldn't! He scowled, and sniffed. Yeah, he had time. Because if him going on about fish and chips was meant to make him feel safe while he got something organized with the welfare, that meant he wouldn't be back for a while. He'd have to actually do the organizing—and the welfare didn't work miracles any more than anyone else did. But what was dead certain, cast-iron, was that he couldn't hang around the flat himself more than an hour or so. He'd got to get on the move or they'd have him in care before he could say 'knife'.

Blast it! Just when he'd got himself sorted out for staying a couple of days till he'd thought things through, this had happened, and it was turfing him out. The nosey, prying, clever, bloody, policeman! All rotten eyes, he was. All over the flat. And a liar to his teeth. You couldn't trust him. There was no way you could trust a man who told you lies the way he did—like yesterday, with that 'sooner he starts his sentence' stuff. Everyone round here knew remand inside counted off your sentence. The rotten lying pig!

Suddenly he punched and kicked his hatred into the hard settee, rocking it. And then, just as suddenly, he stopped, red in the dirty face, and he got on with what he had to do.

82

He took off his trainers and laced up a long pair of Doctor Martin boots; he found a jumper and a fur-lined bomber-jacket; then he ran through into the kitchen and put the baked beans and the cheese into a plastic bag. He rattled in the drawer by the sink for a pointed vegetable knife to stick down his sock, then he gulped down a mug of water, pulled out the plug from the fire and raced out of the flat, not looking back, slamming the door behind him.

But he'd only gone three or four paces when he pulled himself up, his stomach turned. Was his key still round his neck? Yes! Thank Christ for that! Because he wasn't clearing off to sleep rough for ever: only for a night or two, till he could sneak back when the panic was over. And beyond that, now, he wasn't prepared to plan. A hell of a lot could happen in a couple of days, he told himself. And it already bloody had, hadn't it?

The sewer-bank, Ronnie realized, was a good way of getting across the borough. There were no cars on it. The police couldn't patrol that long hump from the comfort of a panda car: and while they could man it where it crossed the roads, they couldn't cruise up behind anyone on it without being seen or heard. They'd have to walk up there: it ran like a bridge across a dangerous estuary, and that made it fairly safe for Ronnie. But he also discovered that when you were looking for good places to come back to and spend the night—like thick bushes, or dips, or empty houses—you couldn't find them, because they just didn't seem to be there. In films, O.K.: in films kids had all sorts of fancy places away from everyone: camps, and barns, and caves: but in real life they weren't there: there was nothing dark enough or thick enough or private enough to hide yourself in. Ronnie saw for himself what Bernie Bradshaw could probably have told him: modern outlaws—villains on the run, or illegal immigrants—had a hard time of it if they didn't have family or friends to help them.

After an hour Ronnie found himself by Cyprus Creek,

because that was where the sewer-bank went, and, like with the railways, you had to go where the tracks took you. Still searching among the desolation for a place to sleep later on, he wandered up-river towards the free ferry. He didn't really have a plan. Keeping on the move and keeping free until nightfall, then getting his head down somewhere would do; then probably the same the next day, and perhaps the next, till it was safe to get back to the flat. And by then it was highly likely something would have happened. The trouble was, he thought, he wasn't used to this sort of thing, planning things out, and all that. He never knew what would happen next week, or next year, or anything. He always had enough to do just to keep his head up for now.

Meanwhile, he could do worse than jump on the ferry, he reckoned. There was sweet Fanny Adams around here, only mud and slippery wood, and stink. And no one took much notice of you on the ferry; he'd found that out the week before. You didn't belong on one side of the river, or the other; and the welfare wouldn't look for you there. And at least you could park your bum for a bit....

Ronnie set off in the new direction and eventually he found himself on the rail of the Woolwich ferry, a lonely figure beneath the crowded vehicle deck, going nowhere. And only then, as the vessel throbbed its rhythm into his chest, did he begin to cry. He didn't howl, or snivel, or rub his eyes with his knuckles. He just cried over the side like being sick, tears that he didn't check or wipe, letting his misery drop in the way of some primitive animal giving birth without fuss: a sad fact of life. His rotten mum. His stupid dad. The violent Bradshaws. The school. Kingsland. They'd all done bloody marvels for him, between the lot of them, hadn't they? There wasn't a one of them he could trust. All out for themselves, they were. Not one of them gave a toss for Ronnie Webster, except perhaps Steve, and he'd never been able to be trusted after he'd knocked back the second glass. And even that was done for now, after the reading card mess up, him seeming to let Steve down, leaving Steve hating him.

There was something about being on the ferry at sea level, something about the wide flatness, free of close buildings and anything overhanging, which helped him to get things out at last. And with the clarity which follows tears he suddenly saw how it had been. As he stared morosely out at the water he realized that he knew damned well who'd done that card thing. Nor did it come as a surprise, because really he'd known all along. There was only one who'd had the chance, and now he was beginning to see the reason. Val. His mum. His rotten mum. She'd done it. No doubt about that.

The six young Cypriots in Coral Island Fish Bar were already run off their feet and D.I. Kingsland had five minutes to wait.

Dave Jones, waiting with him for a lift, leant on the counter patting his moustache and asked, in a confidential, knowing, voice, 'Chips for chat, is it, then, guv? You and the boy?'

'Eh?'

'Grub to get him talking? You give him his supper, gain his confidence with a bit of kindness, and he lets drop one or two things we need to know....'

Johnnie Kingsland stopped tapping the counter top with the edge of his pound note and looked round, frowning, at the younger man. 'Eh?' he said again. 'No, don't be bloody daft....'

'Oh. Sorry, guv. It just seemed a good idea to me....'

'No,' said Kingsland mildly. 'God, no....'

The silence prickled like gorse between them, a momentary awkwardness they'd get round, until eventually, 'Please?' asked an assistant, and cod-and-chips twice was deftly wrapped in thin paper. Then, with little more being said at all, Kingsland dropped Jones off at East Ham underground and turned the car towards Kingston House.

So that was how it looked! Stupid of him to have told anyone what he was doing. Well, to be fair, it probably did seem as if he had to be doing it for what he could get out of it. He couldn't blame Jones for thinking that. He couldn't take the pride he did in his reputation for digging away till he unearthed what he wanted if he was going to feel sore when someone thought he was doing just that. He'd never put anything in an office collecting box in his career, so why should anyone think he was being generous now?

He got out of his car, holding the suppers away from his clothes.

Stevie Webster might be the key to the connecting door between the Bradshaws and the City East raid, but no one would stoop this low to use it, playing on the distress of a kid whose mother had just walked out on him, would they?

The greasy meal was too hot to hold and he switched hands, shivering as he entered the dank hallway of the flats.

No, it was just the kid, being on his own like that, miserable and scared, that had done it. A bit of supper was nothing. Tomorrow would be different; they'd get back to digging again; but tonight, after that terrible note the kid had had, Stevie Webster wouldn't even get mentioned.

Johnnie Kingsland rang the bell of Ronnie's flat, and waited for sounds of life as the chips began to cool.

After that big school dinner Ronnie felt hungrier now than he had on those days when he'd bunked off and nicked just a bar of chocolate from the market. Or perhaps it was the up and down of the ferry-boat, he thought, as he made his second trip across to Woolwich. Sickness and hunger could easily be mistaken for one another. He crammed some crumbly cheese into his mouth, but he couldn't get it down. He'd have to nick some Coke when he got off. As for the baked beans—when you hadn't brought a stinking opener all they were good for was slinging at someone! Ronnie shook the sucking contents as if he were setting a fuse then he lobbed the can at the heaving water. It sank instantly, disappearing quicker than anything he'd ever seen go before. He shivered, and flapping his plastic bag, he turned away from the rail and walked round the boat.

Down in the spartan passenger lounges there were hardly ever many people, not even in the rush-hour home: it was quicker for the able-bodied to walk under the foot tunnel. But up on the vehicle deck there was not a metre of wasted space as cars, vans, and container lorries were packed on like planes on an aircraft carrier. The short crossing provided a few minutes of calm reflection as the drivers switched off their motoring concentration and were floated across London's wide divide. 'A floating pit-stop,' Steve had called it.

As much as a gathering headache and the nausea inside him would allow, Ronnie was thinking, too. Woolwich lay ahead; 'the other side of the water'; South London, where no one would be on the look-out for a kid answering his description. Just as the East End had the Bradshaws they had their own gangs; and both lots left each other alone, the welfare, police and all. So crossing over had a lot of advantages. Getting off the ferry over there wouldn't be at all a bad idea tonight. He could have a quick search round for somewhere to get his aching head down, and, like he'd thought, he'd come back in a few days when they'd all given up looking.

The ferry captain nudged Woolwich gently, and as the hydraulic road descended on to the deck the vehicle engines revved into life and Ronnie pushed himself back off the rail. Yeah, he'd go. He'd definitely get off this time and see what chances came his way. Anyway, he could always come back, couldn't he?

The tide was out so the slope was steep, and Ronnie walked slowly up the ramp of road. After several crossings the ground seemed to move beneath his feet in its firmness,

and suddenly, like walking into cold shadow, all the possibilities of finding a secret hide-out faded as he felt the reality
of Tuesday afternoon in his legs again. It was just the same
in the swimming coach. Thoughts—even terrifying remind-
ers about Charlie Whitelaw's stitched back—seemed to
run on oil when you were moving, and then crashed into the
ground when you stopped. Perhaps old Lessor would've
taught him to read if she'd done it on a bus. Perhaps that
was why Steve only ever worked properly when he was
behind the wheel of a car.

And then Ronnie saw the coach. Almost as if his thoughts
were passing before him he saw the blue and grey of Charlie
Whitelaw's thirty-two seater edging down the ramp towards
the emptied ferry-boat. There was no mistaking the matt
finish of the spray job; and there was no mistaking the sort
of run it was doing: school kids, coming back from a trip
somewhere: all sitting up straight, no fighting in the back
seat, no standing up and shouting through the top windows
at the lorry drivers. No, that was Charlie's coach all right.
And the sight of it stopped Ronnie like a firm hand on the
shoulder.

Charlie Whitelaw had said some strange things the morning before, really weird, and Ronnie hadn't given them
much thought in all the upset of the past two days: but the
sight of the familiar coach in those unfamiliar surroundings
suddenly gave him a strange sense of comfort: and he was
surprised to find that instead of being reminded of the big
man's back and Bernie Bradshaw's threats, he was thinking
about the coach driver's words. And now it hit him. 'I'm on
your side, as it happens....' Christ, yes! Now Ronnie
thought he understood. Charlie had known about Val,
hadn't he? He'd had word, and he'd told him in advance.
The only trouble was, Ronnie hadn't been listening
properly then. 'I'm on your side, as it happens....'

Ronnie sniffed, and stared down into the brown, frothing,
water: a narrow gap where a kid his size could slip and never

be seen again. He shuddered. There was a hell of a lot could happen to a kid on his own round here.

A man with a limp skirted awkwardly round Ronnie, and muttered; and the line of vehicles edged on to the ramp until the barrier came down across the road. And still Ronnie stood, staring into the water. Then he moved. He suddenly turned and ran urgently back down the ramp on to the ferry again.

It seemed crazy, but he had an idea where he might go.

8

Ronnie knew where Charlie's coach yard was because he'd been there with his dad. Several times, when Steve had been filling in with an honest day's work, running pub parties to the races or old people to a knees-up down at Southend, Ronnie had gone to the yard to see him off. He'd never got close enough to wave—even if his family had been the waving sort—but from a distance he'd often been down there to see Steve hang his jacket over the driver's seat before he'd slunk off back home. It was down on Manorway marshes, surrounded by the flat stumps of departed prefabs: a tall, sliced house, which looked as if it had once been intended as part of a long terrace, with a small muddy yard by the side. It was surrounded by a narrow belt of green, where someone had once kept donkeys, and everyone called it 'The Farm'. But within the enclosure, which still seemed unnecessarily small in all the surrounding space, instead of animals there were the coaches: the forty-one seater and the thirty-two, which went, and the old twenty-nine, which didn't.

By the time Ronnie got there, sick with fatigue, the smaller coach he'd seen on the ferry was in the yard, with the gate padlocked across the tracks; while from somewhere under the side of the house a dog barked a frayed warning from the end of a short rope. Frowning under his headache, Ronnie began to feel a hopeless doubt about coming here. It was stupid, all a mistake. The bloke was probably as bent as all the rest of them, whatever he said. Who was he kidding? Why not just flop down in that ditch opposite for a couple of hours? That was favourite, because if you didn't trust anyone, you couldn't get let down, could you? He pushed the padlock chain, ready to turn and go when it didn't yield; but it gave—just enough for his thin stick of body to poke itself through the gate—and, almost disappointed, he pushed himself in.

He found himself up against a warm radiator grill, the wide front of the coach looming over him. His head was filled with the mulled smell of hot anti-freeze; and he breathed in deeply. He stayed there, close to the vehicle, and his spirits picked up a bit as he experienced the warm comfort of being close to something Steve would have understood.

But the dog was barking falsetto in its excitement, and a door slammed.

'Belt up!' There was a sudden yelp and then a claw-on-concrete scratching before the dog bravely began again. 'Who's there, then? Come on, let's 'ave you!'

It was Charlie Whitelaw, and he definitely wasn't pleased about being brought out. But all the same, he was round to the front of the coach like lightning, and Ronnie's second sudden decision to turn and clear off out of it hadn't a hope in hell of working. He'd only managed to get his plastic bag back through the gap when the brass buckle of a broad belt levelled up with him, and the big square face was looking down, frowning; frightening. Then, as Ronnie stared, his heart pounding like a rabbit's, Charlie Whitelaw recognized who it was, and started chewing on his supper again.

'Stevie Webster's boy!' he said.

Ronnie looked at the big man through eyes which had become defensive slits again.

'Done it, then, 'as she?'

A tough frown from Ronnie; he didn't give a toss what she'd done; but he nodded all the same.

'Come on then, son. Come in the 'ouse.'

Charlie took Ronnie's plastic bag and led the way down the narrow space between the coaches, chewing noisily on his mouthful of steak. 'Belt up, I said!' he shouted at the young alsation which had become frantic at seeing Ronnie, and he left the boy to skirt the rope's arc while he held the house door marked 'Strictly Private' wide open.

'Elsie!' he called. 'It's Stevie Webster's boy....' There was no audible reply.

Any passage or corridor which Charlie Whitelaw was in was narrow, and the passage which divided the front from the back of the house was no exception, with its wall rubshined at shoulder height: it was neither clean, nor dirty, and the whirled carpet had been flattened by the big man's feet, in and out on business. The door on their immediate right was ajar, and Ronnie could see an old-fashioned desk with spikes of oily chits; and over-all there was the mixed smell of engine grease, alsation, and chips; an air of honest graft rather than easy crooked money.

The cooking fat curled at Ronnie as the door on his left opened and a small gipsy-looking woman with long black hair and a lined forehead stood in the gap.

'Who?' she asked.

'Ronnie. Stevie Webster's Ronnie. I told you, didn't I?'

'Yes, you did,' she said, as if that were neither here nor there.

'Well, he'll want a bit of supper....'

'And he'll have it.' She turned her back on them and addressed the cooker. 'Come on in, then, son, and stick your bum down on one of them chairs.' Ronnie sidled into the room. 'Egg and chips?'

Ronnie nodded and muttered a 'Yeah' that no one could hear, and nothing more was said for some time as Ronnie sat up and Charlie made a fresh, lightning-knifed, assault on his huge steak.

There was nothing instant about the meal Elsie had cooked, except, perhaps, the speed with which she served him. There was nothing pre-cooked or take-away about it. Egg and chips was two eggs, perfectly fried, pricked and running hot and yellow over a mound of crisp golden chips, with a grilled tomato on the side and two slices of soft bread and butter for mopping up. A mug of sweet tea and a sugar-rough doughnut followed swiftly behind it, while Elsie moved about in silence and Charlie drank two cups of tea and pretended to read the *Sun*.

Ronnie ate it all up: the food, the comfort of the kitchen, and the sudden and strange sense of not having to listen or look out for anyone for five minutes. It was like a tranquillizing drug taking effect after a long pain.

'Well,' Charlie said at last, folding the paper small, 'it's a sad thing, a very sad thing, but it's 'appened, and that's that.'

The sink filled with hot water and Elsie went out to throw something to eat at the dog.

'I s'pose you know where Val's gone?'

Ronnie's face felt strangely numb, and he shook his head. He didn't frown and he didn't shrug. Perhaps it was a sort of shock that had set in, but he felt whoozy enough to hear the man say anything about anybody, and not care.

'Bradshaw,' said Charlie Whitelaw, flicking the boy with an eye to see how he took it. 'Bernie Bradshaw. She fancies the high life Stevie ain't giving her any more now he's packed up the racing motors....'

Ronnie stared at the table. This was his mother the man was telling him about. And still he felt numb: but it wasn't with shock: it was with fatigue, mental as much as physical. Charlie could have said she'd gone off with any high-up in the land.

'Oh, yeah?' Ronnie's voice didn't seem to be his own.

'Yeah. Bernie Bradshaw: which, as you know, 'as its problems. But I'm fond of your old man, Ronnie, 'e's a bit special to me, boy . . . and besides, I know the feeling, son. . . .' Charlie stared at the table himself. 'So you stick your 'ead down 'ere for a bit, eh—till we get things sorted out? Right?'

Charlie looked up and began unfolding his *Sun* again. Ronnie stared, and he might have nodded. The man seemed all right indoors: not like he was on the coach at all. He'd done right to come, and he'd be stupid to go now, wouldn't he? Not for a bit. He drew in a deep, deep, breath, something his body suddenly seemed to demand. Especially when he was feeling rough like this, numb, and a bit sick, and all of a sudden ready to drop down dead with tiredness.

Eyes staring, he drew in another deep breath, desperately seeking air like a sick fish. God, he felt funny. Real . . . funny. . . .

'Where's the lav?' he heard himself say. And then the kitchen floor seemed to come up, slowly, gently, to meet him.

The next day was limbo. It didn't count for Ronnie; Wednesday didn't exist, as if it had been taken—beginning, middle, and end—off the calendar. It was like the day after an accident, or after the feverish onset of illness, when daylight comes and goes in unconsciousness, when brief images seen from the deep pillow might be real or might be dreamt. The purple curtains were drawn, and the voices of the fleeting figures were subdued. Full cups came in hot and went out cold. Doors opened and closed in the distance and engines revved in some other unbelievable existence where people were up and about. And surrounding the scattered islands of hazy consciousness was the deep pleasure of sleep, total comfort on back, on side, on front, where every satisfaction was fulfilled. Ronnie Webster's overstressed mind and body took the opportunity to catch up.

A second night came and went, and then the daylight of another morning awakened Ronnie to a full and refreshed consciousness.

''Ere you are, son. Cup o' tea.'

Ronnie looked around him, somehow not surprised to be in a strange bed. He was in a small room: bed, iron fireplace, dressing-table and sash window: a homely sort of place, in an old-fashioned way.

Charlie Whitelaw, in his shaving vest, was leaning over the bed.

''Ow you feeling, Ron? Bit better this morning?' His voice quavered in its unaccustomed softness, and Ronnie felt strangely uncomfortable, as if he didn't deserve this treatment. In the coach the teacher bottled and scraped at this man—and here the man was bringing him tea, opening his curtains, looking at him with one eye as if the way he felt mattered.

'Yeah,' he said, sitting up quickly to please.

'Good boy. Well, get that tea down you and come on downstairs. Elsie's got a pan o' bacon going. . . . '

'Yeah. O.K.'

Charlie went back to the door. 'You done right,' he said. 'Coming 'ere. . . . '

Ronnie nodded, and swallowed. Then he sniffed. It was very likely true; he wanted it to be; but he'd better be careful; he'd never gone overboard on the strength of just a couple of smiles.

The big man went and Ronnie got out of bed—to the sudden shock of the free feel of his own nakedness. God, what was this? Who the hell had undressed him? Charlie? Elsie? He only ever went down to his pants himself, undressing; and not as far as that, washing. But he could see himself here as white and clean all over as after swimming; and, without the cling of chlorine, that was something new. He shivered in his exposure, like a shorn lamb, and he reached for his pants. No need to bother washing now, then. He had to look at the pants twice, though. They were his, and yet they weren't, shiny-ironed and a shade lighter than usual. And the shirt looked smart, the stains faded when he looked for them, and the torn bits sewn. This was a hell of a lot more trouble than his old lady had ever taken, he thought. At home it all went in the machine together, except her own stuff, and it all came out a sort of grey. And then you wore it. The iron was only for sticking sexy patches on her jeans.

Ronnie had a sudden vision of her ironing for Bernie Bradshaw, standing up behind the ironing-board with a drink on the mantelpiece, laughing, and doing for the fat crook what she wouldn't do for Steve or himself. God, when you thought about it all it was so bloody hard to believe. Bernie Bradshaw. *Bradshaw!* The old enemy. The traitor who'd seen to Steve! Ronnie went hot, and clenched his fists by his side. The cow! But it couldn't last. There was no chance....

He didn't know the house, but the bacon, with a smell as strong as sound, called him in the right direction: left, along a landing of secret doors, and then down a narrow flight of turning stairs to the corridor below. He remembered where the kitchen was now. Anyway, Charlie must have been listening for him: he appeared immediately and beckoned the boy into the room with a jerk of his grey head and a matey wink.

Now Ronnie could see why coach drivers rarely ate sandwiches on trips out. Breakfasts like Elsie's weren't meant to be followed too closely by anything else to eat. Four pink rashers crouched hot on the plate, with two fried eggs, a burst sausage too big for its own skin, tomatoes and mushrooms heaped like baked beans, and on a plate in the middle of the table, stacked up towards him, were thick layers of buttered bread. It was very different from his own half-hearted cereal. And that was the trouble. For now, in the private world of someone else's breakfast, he suddenly felt acutely embarrassed. What was he doing here? He shouldn't be sitting in on this, should he? He ought to be sharing whatever Steve was having.

Elsie, who seemed to waste words as if they were pound notes, simply said, 'Eat up, son. Do you good.' And Ronnie did, with his head down, pleased to have something to do. But he still felt hot and red, trying to think of what to say; and he ate noisily, swallowing whole mouthfuls without chewing in his awkwardness. He gulped some tea, and burped, and bent his head lower over his food.

The driver was sitting opposite, an uncreased *Sun* in one hand, forking in whole curled rashers with the other, levering from the elbow on the white wood table. But he had an eye for Ronnie all the time, and when the boy's plate was clean and Ronnie didn't know where to look, he laid the paper down and, using his fork as a pointer, he told him straight.

'Right, my old China; now today you're goin' to school. . . .'

Ronnie frowned and his eyes narrowed. What was all this now?

'It's all right, Ron, don't get the 'ump, son. We're not shooting you out. Are we, Elsie?' Elsie, facing the stove, shook her head silently. 'No, we're playing it clever.' He leaned closer, across the bread. 'Look,' he said, 'with Steve inside, and your old woman left 'ome, the natural thing is to shoot you in a council 'ome, for your own protection. It's the natural thing because they make sure you're looked after and you go to school. And if you're missing school you're not being properly took care of in their eyes. Right? But,' he drew the word out for emphasis, 'if you turn up at the school, clean and decent, regular to time an' behaving yourself, they'll say, "Someone's lookin' after him all right. 'E must be in good 'ands." And they're so pushed for places in these 'omes—ain't they, Els?—it'll suit them down to the ground to leave you 'ere. See?' He stared an answering nod out of Ronnie, who had followed all that, but who was still puzzling desperately to sort out Charlie's angle in doing all this. 'Now, listen, they know me up the school through the coaches, but in case that ain't enough all you've got to tell them is you're staying with relations till your mum and dad sort themselves out. All right?'

That seemed O.K., Ronnie thought. Anyway, let things ride. Blow working everything out. See how things went.

'You can say you're with ... your grandparents,' Charlie said, quavering again. 'Your grandad and your ...'

There was a pause.

'Grandmother,' Elsie said to the circling tea.

'Your grandmother,' Charlie repeated. He relaxed a bit, and sniffed. 'I dunno. "Nan" sounds more like it, Elsie....'

Elsie shrugged, as Ronnie might. 'He can please himself,' she said, pushing second mugs across. 'Please yourself, son.'

'Well, say whatever seems right,' Charlie said. 'They won't go into it; not unless they've got more time than I give 'em credit for. Now, you know your address, don't you? "The Farm". And here's your dinner money.' He dug a big paw into his pocket and tossed a fifty pence piece across. 'An' I'll give you a run up in the coach—it's on my way today—but tomorrow you can get used to the 101. Right, my old son?' Then he laughed, and slopped his own tea. "Grandson", I should say, eh? He laughed again, but it sounded pushed out to Ronnie, a bit like the jollying-along people do in a crisis.

Charlie folded his *Sun* for his pocket while Ronnie scraped back his chair. But he was frowning again. Things moved so quick! he thought. He put the fifty pence in his pocket, and he wrinkled his nose as if he were short-sighted. Then he sniffed. So, his dad had gone inside, his mum had

97

done a bunk, and now he'd got a gran and a grandad! Well, he'd never had one of them before, so that was something new. But lurking somewhere near as well were the others: Kingsland, the copper, and Bernie Bradshaw, his old lady's boy-friend. And neither of them was going to sit back and let him quietly enjoy being someone's grandson: not till someone got done properly by the police for the football job.

No wonder he had the burps. God, he had a hell of a lot more puzzling out to do—when he felt a bit more like it.

Manjit was making her own puzzled way to school that Thursday morning, bumping into people and being sworn at as her mind worried at her own problems, at something she'd seen and heard the night before. She felt elated and dejected by turn, her spirits rising each time she saw a turbanned head, sinking when a policeman came into sight.

She hadn't been meant to hear. Now she knew that Sarinder and their mother had been keeping everything from her for this very reason, preferring her to make the best of her father's absence rather than worry, and perhaps run the risk of having her high hopes dashed. But there had been news brought to them, something important to be passed on, and the brother of whoever had called before had come this time, earlier than the other because he was on his way to something special, he'd said: and so Manjit had seen and heard, and noticed the slight, glamorous-looking woman sitting outside in the motor car, smoking hard and looking slowly about her like a film star in a slum.

Satya was watching television when the bell rang, and Manjit ran in to sit next to her, to be part of it this time, if she could. She switched off the set when the bald man came in and she sat with her hands in her lap like her mother, while the men transacted their business in the bay window.

'I'm doin' my brother a favour,' Bernie Bradshaw said, not sure what the boy knew of their names, 'calling in for 'im: 'e's a bit tied up tonight.' He sat back in the chair as if he owned the place, lighting a big cigar leisurely and looking to be in no way concerned about the lady waiting outside. Opposite him Sarinder perched on the edge of his chair, alert, like a bird sitting too close to a basking alligator.

'Do you have some news to tell me, please?' Sarinder asked.

Bernie looked down the room at the two females while he got the cigar going. 'They all right?' he asked. 'Them no speakie to no one?'

Sarinder looked hard at Manjit, and then he shook his head. 'It's in all our interests not to speak to anyone of this, I tell you, sir....'

Leaning forward, Bernie blew smoke in his face. 'Yeah, you're dead right there, son,' he said with an edge. 'Because most of all it ain't in my interest, you could say. An' don't no one forget it, neither.' Then he sheathed his voice and sat back again. 'Well, 'e says it's all set up, if the money's right.' He paused. Then, sharply again, 'Well, is it, or not? Only if it ain't I can't tell you no more....'

Sarinder got up quickly and went out of the room, returning a few seconds later with a folded blue envelope. He glanced briefly at his mother, then: 'There's a quarter of it here, like we arranged before. My father will have the rest with him.'

Manjit's hand shot to her mouth to cover a cry of surprise. But if Bernie Bradshaw saw her he took no notice.

'Boulogne, on the coast,' he said. ''E says they've got their own set-up to get them that far. We just bring 'em over the 'ard bit, into the land of plenty, you could say.' He pocketed the envelope. 'I take it this is right?' He patted his pocket and nodded with Sarinder as he smiled. 'Right, now listen: you'll get a picture postcard put through your door one day soon, with a date on it and details of a week-end trip to Paris. Old age pensioners, in a coach. Pretend you 'elp out with 'em sometimes, voluntary stuff, and write and

99

tell your old man, your father, right? And you tell 'im all about it; the date they come back, the Sunday, and the name of a little caff I'll give you where they'll 'ave their tea; outside Boulogne. Make it good, wrap it all round in any old rubbish you like in case it gets seen. But you make sure you get all the details in. Because if 'e ain't at the caff when the coach gets back to Boulogne, we can't bring 'im back, can we?' He looked down the room again, and this time he dropped his voice a bit, like an undertaker talking money. 'The only other little thing is, your father, right, 'e's got to look Algerian, you know, their dark workers—like our Irish—just while 'e's swanning round France. So it's no beard, short 'air, no thingummy on top, get it?' Sarinder nodded, saying nothing. 'But 'ow you get that bit in your letter's down to you. I know cutting your 'air off's a bit 'ard for you foreign gentlemen, but it's worth a sacrifice, eh? To get back 'ome....'

He got up and dusted ash off his light blue trousers on to the carpet. Sarinder got up, too, and he was still nodding when the two fat pink hands suddenly shot out and gripped his face, hurting, pressing his cheeks on to his teeth harder and harder in accentuation of the caution the man was hissing. 'An' we don't tell a living bloody soul, right?' He let the youth go, then cuffed the black head playfully before getting out a big handkerchief and flamboyantly wiping his hands. 'I don't know the exact date or time, but it's Boulogne for definite. And it's highly likely to be a coach firm round 'ere. Whitelaws. And they won't be no more pleased than me if word gets out. Savvy? But you'll get all the details in a couple o' days.' He smiled down the room at Satya as if she were a deaf mute of six. 'Don't get up, love,' he said: and he went out to the car, running lightly round the front of it for the benefit of the waiting passenger.

The car eased away, laughing, leaving behind a tense house in which a lot of hurried explanations were suddenly being given to a shaking girl.

'You knew, didn't you? Or you guessed....' Sarinder said. 'You wanted to hear, so you've heard. And now you must forget it all, because that man and his brother can do us great harm. And they can decide whether to bring our father back or not....'

So Manjit had hardly slept, and when she had, cat-napping around dawn, her father had come to her in her dreams—with his hair cut off and his beard shaved, the loved and the familiar face almost terrifying in its changed state, exposed and vulnerable, like a dead man seen without his teeth. And not long after that she had heard the door shut quietly—as Sarinder had gone to the Gurdwara to pray. And yet for all that worrying and lying awake, here she was going to school still without any of her feelings really sorted out. It was a big mistake, she decided, ever to believe that there always had to be a moment when you could make up your mind about something. There were problems like this which would remain unresolved inside your head until they had been resolved *for* you, in reality.

'Mind out!'

A woman had stopped to read the collection times on a pillar box and Manjit had nudged her as she passed.

'I'm sorry....'

'Yeah, I should bloody-well think so an' all!' The woman went on, complaining to a man about the Indian problem while she posted her letter; and for the thousandth time Manjit thought about the letter Sarinder would write to her father in Delhi; and she pictured him travelling, having to cut off his hair in Europe, doing something he was com-mitted against doing religiously. Would he do it, in order to get back illegally into Britain? She imagined him huddled like an animal under the seat of a coach, pushed about, treated badly, perhaps being arrested, imprisoned.... Then she remembered all the Sundays; the family days; the Sikh things they did—the visits to the Gurdwara, sitting round together while her father read from the Granth, the sweetmeats after the meetings; and the English things—walking together in the park, eating ice-cream, feeding the ducklings that by now would be mother ducks; all the being together of her family. And she didn't know what she wanted her father to do, how she would advise him, if she could.

Manjit turned a corner and reached the school. She'd come a long way and seen so many visions inside her head that she was confused now, and she began to doubt whether any of what she'd seen and heard the night before could really be true. Perhaps she'd dreamt the whole thing. But as she crossed the last road she was made suddenly aware that it couldn't all be dismissed that easily. For pulling up outside the school gate was a coach, letting someone off; just one; and she saw that it was the spiteful one, Ronnie, the boy whose sad letter she had read two or three days before; and she saw, too, that the coach bringing him had a name along the side which she could read. 'Whitelaw'. And yet another strand was added to the knot of her confusion.

9

From the careful blank look on Miss Neame's face Ronnie read that they'd been talking about him in the staff room, and he quite expected Wendy Camp to be sent off straight away with a note to Mrs. Monks, all secret service. But the teacher didn't seem to want to make anything of him being away again; nothing special, anyway.

'Ah, Webster,' said Miss Neame. 'Here you are.' She held out her hand and shut her arched eyes as she always did, her signal for being given the absence note she knew she wouldn't get.

Ronnie put it in her hand, and the unexpected contact made her jump, as if someone had done something he shouldn't in the underground.

'Oh!' she said. 'Ah. *Thank* you.'

She opened it and Ronnie sat down and stared at the wall, kicking aimlessly at the skirting. He didn't know what it said; just that Elsie had got it out of her overall pocket and given it to him; but he expected it was about her and Charlie being his gran and grandad—and his mum going away.

'Ah, I see....' Miss Neame folded the letter and put it into her handbag, instead of into the back of the register. 'Thank your grandmother, will you?'

Ronnie sniffed and jerked his head—hardly a nod. He looked round defensively to see if anyone was taking any notice, trying to make anything out of him actually having a letter. But he still didn't exist in that room: he could have run up the walls, swung on the lights, ridden Miss Neame piggyback round the desks, and no one would have taken any notice of him. They'd grown up with him, most of them, and he wasn't a laugh, or good at anything; he couldn't fight, they reckoned; he was always the last to be picked for anything; so he came and went on his own, not even noticed enough to give them a bit of amusement. To them he was just a hollow-eyed, grimy, washed-out kid with a runny nose who no one had any time for.

The others got work out. Some mucked about and were ticked off, but after a while the room was quiet and Ronnie went through his token performance of leafing through a Ladybird, while Miss Neame did private things at her desk. But Ronnie had one eye on the class-room door, too, and his mind was filled with the nag of what could happen. Could the welfare just come and take him away? Or would it be Mrs. Monks, the big smile with the strong grip? Or might Charlie have been right, and everything be allowed to stay as it was for a while, until....

Till what? Ronnie asked himself. Till Kingsland let his dad go and Bernie Bradshaw had to do something a bit more definite about him? Because that was what it came down to. That reading card had definitely been put there by Val, not just in his jeans, but hidden somewhere in the car, taking a nice little chance to get Steve out of the way. So if Steve didn't *stay* out of the way, he'd have to be *put* out of it. Or perhaps things would stay like they were till Bradshaw kicked Val out—and she either came crawling home or cleared off with the next one on the list. Ronnie didn't know. He ground his teeth. Hell, everything was so bloody up-and-down it was a wonder he stayed right enough to sit at his desk and even pretend with some of this rubbish; like this stupid book where the bloke and the old woman take the smarmy kids down the seaside in the motor. He gripped it hard, feeling the cover begin to crack. He looked up to see if *she'd* heard—and suddenly he wanted nothing more than to chop it round the back of her fat neck....

But he wouldn't. Especially today. 'Behave yourself,' Charlie Whitelaw had said, 'and they'll probably let you hang on here at "The Farm"....'

He couldn't stop his thoughts, though: and the idea of chopping Miss Neame round the neck grew. It was a pleasant thought and it began to race his heart; his eyes lost their focus and he pursued it with several variations inside his head: doing it with a bigger book, with a big bit of wood, with a heavy, rusty, chopper. But sitting there behind Bernie Bradshaw would be best. Ronnie where he was, and fat Bradshaw at Neames's desk. God, yes! With the rusty axe!

Ronnie swallowed; and he cuffed his nose as it ran. He looked round, his eyes alight. It was a good place to think, to let your ideas out, here in the classroom when someone wasn't rabbiting on. He looked back again at Miss Neame, standing in for Bernie Bradshaw. The axe; a meat-knife; or a squat gun, blue-black in his hand ... SPLAT!

It was the best way, wasn't it? Quick and for good.

THUNK! 'Aaaaaagh!' Well, tell us a better way....

The bell went then, and Ronnie, red and clammy, had to put his violent thoughts away with the Ladybird book. But he'd still got other things to think about, more realistic, real things....

Up in the converted cloakroom Miss Lessor once again had Ronnie's distracted mind to do battle with that Thursday. She knew about the boy, and she was used to him being awkward. But he'd forgotten everything about letters, and she despaired again as his mind seemed unprepared even to register the new set of sound cards. 'Build it,' she said. 'Build it. N...e...t.... I can do it; I can read, I'm all right; I only want your effort for your own sake....' But he wasn't having any.

She couldn't see behind the glazed eyes to the racing thoughts in the circuits of his brain; the Bradshaw circuit, and the Val Webster circuit, and the constant going over the same ground, lap after lap, as the worried mind dictated; Bradshaw and violence, Val Webster and treachery; and then, with a cold lighting-up of the eyes, the accidental image, suddenly remembered, of the girl over there who knew one of his closest secrets.

'Well, leave it, we're wasting each other's time,' Miss Lessor said. And then she turned to the other distracted mind, today the greater disappointment. 'Oh, come on, Manjit, you've done so well up to now.'

The girl was struggling through her book, stumbling over easy words, reading with a lack of fluency which was worse than when she'd first come. But for Manjit, too, printed words weren't important today. There weren't the tears, but this was worse, because by the time she wanted to cry at least she'd know where she was; at least she'd be sure of something, even if it was only the certainty of her own unhappiness. Turmoil, conflict, was worse; it was more draining, it occupied more of you.

And that was how Manjit was as the words froze back into meaningless blocks on the page.

'Oh, come on; you knew "traffic" yesterday; we did all the "tr" words: "train", "trip", "travel", "transport", "trap" ... hundreds of them....'

But Manjit couldn't see Miss Lessor's sense any more than Ronnie could, and eventually the teacher dismissed them early, lighting a cigarette and throwing the Ronson back into her handbag in annoyance. Ronnie's failure she accepted; there wasn't much there to work with; but had Manjit now reached a plateau she was going to find it hard to move off? She looked at the books and the cards on the table: and she began to wonder if it were her, perhaps. Perhaps she needed to find a new approach to their problems. Perhaps she wasn't identifying their problems properly. She scratched her head carefully, and sighed.

Even after all the ups and downs of the past few days it still seemed strange for Ronnie to be deliberately going home to a different house. To walk out of the gate and turn left instead of right was something new; and he felt funny doing it, like having to go into a different shop for his mum when she hadn't paid a bill in the old one. He still looked round about him, but not for the old reason. Val wouldn't let Bradshaw get him, would she? No, it was the welfare he had to look out for, just in case....

He walked along the pavement towards the 101 bus stop. The violence had gone for the time being. A big dinner and a warm, easy, afternoon had slowed the racing images: and having reached a climax in imagining violent ways of dealing with Bernie Bradshaw, now he felt somehow satisfied, and spent: and in a mood approaching contentment he walked along looking at the different shades of the paving stones, seeing the secret patterns in the slabs which people who could read the street names rarely saw.

'Head up, Ronnie; things'll get better, you see.'

God! It was the copper, leaning up against a big tree.

Clear off quick! Turn and run, both together; put his head down, get his arms and legs pumping. Put a block between him and the copper before the man could even lean up off that tree. That was his first instinctive reaction. But no, Ronnie wasn't stupid: and his intelligence, his cunning, overcame his instinct and he stood his ground instead. Why look guilty? He hadn't done anything; and as far as the law was concerned, Charlie was his grandad and he was going back to his proper home. So he sniffed, and scowled at Kingsland with a defiant 'you-can't-touch-me' about the mouth and his hands clenched by his sides.

'You look smart....'

Kingsland meant clean; because that was what Ronnie was. He wasn't one of those kids who dirtied clean clothes in a day, like clean children could: he didn't play enough to get dirty quickly; he got dirty slowly, and he stayed that way: a deep, lengthy grime. But today he was clean. Ronnie shrugged and half turned his head away, but he kept his suspicious eyes riveted on the policeman.

'I came back last night, like I promised I would; on my own. But you weren't there....' He didn't mention the half-hour he'd waited, or the two portions of cold cod and chips he'd tipped out for the birds in Victoria Park.

'Wasn't I?'

'So you're all right, then? Gone to someone in the family, have you?'

Ronnie squinted at him through slit eyes. The copper made him sound like some dog whose owner had died. He sniffed, and blinked.

'Far off? Want a lift?'

Ronnie shook his head. 'Got me bus fare....'

'Oh, that's fine, then. As long as you're O.K.' Kingsland unwrapped a chewing-gum and held it out for Ronnie. 'As a matter of fact I'm going to be a bit pushed myself for a bit. Something's come up—big—and I might be very busy for a few weeks.' He pushed the gum again. 'Which is a shame, because until I can pull someone else for the football job your dad's all we've got: and it won't be long before we have to start bringing more serious charges and ask for more remands in custody.' He said it in a very matter-of-fact tone, the professional aspect which no one could pretend didn't exist. It went with a slight sharpening of his features and longer closings of his thin eyelids. Then he softened his voice. 'But don't forget, if ever I can help, you or your dad, just get a message to me at the nick.' He put the cold gum in his mouth and leant off the tree. 'All right, Ronnie?'

But Ronnie had turned away and was carrying on walking: only now he wasn't looking at the shades in the paving stones, and he wasn't feeling mildly contented any more: now he just wanted to catch that bus and put a good long distance between himself and the rotten law....

The top of the bus was crowded, hot, and smoky, dead with trapped flies and grey-faced passengers. Ronnie found a vacant seat at the front and put his boot up on the ledge, waiting for someone to tell him to take it down: but no one did, not even the conductor, and he was left, like the rest, to the world inside his head.

That creep Kingsland. He'd been dead right not to trust him, with all his talk of cod and chips the other night, and now giving him all that stuff about having to let Steve get done for the football raid. The big pilk! Nothing was what you thought it was. When it came down to it they all had their own angle to look after. Like Val. (He somehow couldn't even think of her as his mum any more.) She had him, she had Steve, and then she cleared off with someone else when it suited her. She did worse than clear off: she even got Steve put inside so she could do it. So he couldn't even trust his own old lady.

He looked down at the Co-op and watched a woman hitting a toddler for tripping over the wheels of the baby's pram. He sniffed. All the same, weren't they? She gave him money, she gave him grub—and that was about the lot, while she went at it working out her own angle! He ground his teeth. The rotten cow. And old mother Neame, and stinking Lessor. He scowled out of the wide pane. If they came up here on the bus they'd probably pretend it wasn't him sitting there—Val and all! Only his dad'd do anything for him. And then not him if he'd had a drink. No, Ronnie thought, the more you thought about it the more you realized you were on your own. So the message was, grab what you wanted for yourself, because no one else cared much. Trust no one; and don't be fooled, like Steve; not by anyone, not by your mum, or anyone—and that included Charlie and Elsie, because they'd got an angle too, 'Grandad' and 'Nan', you could bet on that.

But when Ronnie got in it was hard to see what that angle could be. They sat him up to another huge supper in the kitchen, and then he sat in sniffing silence with them and watched the television programmes till close-down. And when he got up to go to bed Elsie went out and came back into the room with one of her rare words and a new pair of Russian-style pyjamas.

'Catch,' she said, and threw them at him. And Charlie laughed, and said, 'Great, Ron!'

It was the next evening after a boring day at school when Ronnie first thought he was going to see their angle. Charlie waited till they were eating, then, between forkfuls, he put his paper down and made a proposition to the boy.

'Wanna earn yourself a few bob, Ronnie?' He washed the question down with tea and stared earnestly at him, the hard face softened with bacon fat.

Hello, what was this? Well, Ronnie could think of a few possibilities straight off, no trouble. A look-out on a raid? A kid small enough to get through a fanlight? Or a grandson to make things look normal at the dogs? There were millions of things it could be. He'd wondered how long it would be coming; because no one ever did anything for nothing, and now it looked as if he was going to have to start paying for his keep.

Ronnie used a big mouthful of his own to cover a lack of words; but he looked at Charlie and he was surprised by a sudden jaunty wink.

'She's all for giving you a bit of spending money straight out,' Charlie said, as if Elsie weren't just behind him at the sink. 'But I said I reckoned you'd sooner do something for it. Feel a bit useful, eh? Sort of independent....'

Ronnie wrinkled his nose and sniffed. Well, he was dead wrong there. He'd much sooner Charlie just gave it him. Who wouldn't?

'You could give me 'and in the coaches,' he said, wrapping him round with his voice in a matey way. 'End of the day after I'm finished you could give one of 'em a sweep out, you know, the old dustpan and brush touch, tip the ash-trays out an' clear up the mess.' He waited while Ronnie did a lot of swallowing; thinking about it. 'An' it'd be 'elp with my back. All that bending does me....'

Ronnie looked at him hard.

'Fifty p a coach,' said Charlie, 'an' extra when we wash 'em out an' hose 'em down. Be nice to 'ave something to jingle in your pocket, won't it?'

'Yeah....' Ronnie shrugged. 'If you like....' Well, there wasn't any saying no, was there?

'Right, then, I'll show you what to do over the week-end. Sunday morning, all right?'

'Yeah.'

'Right.'

Well, back or no back, Charlie had an angle, Ronnie thought. And when he found out what it was would be the time to make his mind up whether to go or to stay.

Saturday dragged, with Charlie out on a run to the races, and Elsie busy with her back to the room, at the stove or the sink. Ronnie watched a lot of television on the old black-

and-white set, and found himself thinking about the big colour set standing idle in the flat, wondering if they could pick it up sometime, if they ever went up in the coach for some of his clothes. He might ask about it, Ronnie thought. But when Charlie came in that night with some odds and ends of clothes, all new and not bad, he kept quiet. Besides, he might need it back in the flat himself sometime, he told himself. You never knew. You had to plan more than one jump ahead....

Elsie didn't say much. But she was all right, as far as he could tell. She did her cooking and her cleaning, and she didn't seem to want much else except her cigarettes—which seemed to be her only interest after their bellies. But since he'd never demanded much himself he could think of a lot to be said for being like Elsie.

The only other thing he fancied doing was sitting up in the old coach and pretending to drive it. But it was locked, and the dog still had a go at him so he didn't go in and out too much on his own anyway: and besides, he'd have felt stupid sitting up there like a kid. He'd never got used to playing games. So he drifted out of one chair and into another on the Saturday.

On the Sunday, though, Charlie started off by showing him all the ropes. He showed him the vehicle log books and the drivers' records, and the paperwork to do with petrol and mileage: and Ronnie had to take his word for all that: but topping up the water and the long batteries in the lockers along the side was more in his line, and he was interested to see how to lift the engine cover from inside the coach and dip for oil. On top of that while they were up there Charlie took time to show him what all the switches worked, and he played the radio, and let him blow a raspberry into the microphone for telling people where they were. And almost against his will Ronnie found he hadn't enjoyed himself so much for a hell of a long time. Outside school his life seemed to have been like Saturday, all chairs, out of one and into another, watching the box or listening to the stereo. The odd bit of tagging along with Steve, or the odd tale of a great race, well, they happened from time to time; but none of it had ever involved him. Not before the football job, anyhow. But not like this. This was great, he thought. Charlie really got a kick out of showing him; they got greasy together; and for a long while that morning Ronnie even forgot to wonder what Charlie's angle was in all this.

They cleaned out the coach after.

There was a slick way of doing everything; even cleaning a coach out had its tricks of the trade, Ronnie found. Ashtrays into the dustpan, one-two, one-two; stiff brush across the seats; soft broom into the centre gangway; then a quick sweep down the coach, off the steps, and the whole lot into a bucket standing under the door.

'Ten minutes,' said Charlie, 'when it's dry and no one's been sick. But you can 'ave as long as you like most nights, an' 'alf-an-hour when I've got an evening run....'

Ronnie sniffed, and almost smiled. 'Ta,' he said.

But it took him over forty-five minutes on the Monday.

'That's all right, Ron; don't you worry, mate,' Charlie said. 'You'll soon get the 'ang of it. Anyway, you done a good job, I can tell you....'

But on Tuesday Ronnie thought he'd do without the sympathy and get on with it straight away, as soon as the coach came in. Charlie was in his little office, deep in dockets, so Ronnie didn't bother him for the locker key. He knew where it was, up in the coach. He skirted the dog widely and got out the things, manoeuvred the tall broom to lie along the back seat and with a few sidelong glances at himself working in the reflecting windows he started on the ash-trays and the seat covers with the dustpan and brush.

It wasn't very dirty. Charlie had been driving it himself, and nobody took liberties with Charlie's ash-trays; but there was the odd sweet wrapping, screwed defiantly small, which had to be got out. After the ash-trays Ronnie cleaned the back seats with the stiff brush, then he glanced down the coach at the clock. Ten to two. That wasn't right: stopped, hadn't it? But he definitely wasn't taking so long tonight. He'd be done in good time for Elsie's supper. He began to feel pleased with himself; a small tickle of pride in the pit of his stomach; something to take the place of worrying about him and Steve and the Bradshaws for five minutes.

He worked on, ash-trays into bin, brush along the seats, his mind fully occupied now with counting them off as he went, unable to think of anything else till he was done. Five seats finished along the back, then the next four done; that was nine; then another four, that was twelve, no, thirteen; then another four, that was....

He stopped there, looking down. Erk! Oh, lovely! Forget the counting! Filthy berks! This was going to hold him up something rotten! Just as he was doing all right....

Down there on the floor, under the seat in front of the wheel arch, were the mouldering remains of a squashed apple, gone-off and all soft like the last one in a bowl, something chucked out of a bag and trodden into the lino. Ronnie scowled, and swore. He'd have to get this up with his fingers. Or leave it. Christ, he'd like to thump who'd done that!

Over by the house the dog suddenly started a choking whine. Charlie was coming. Oh, God! And he'd wanted to be done before Charlie saw the coach. Just his rotten luck! Well, at least he could see him at it....

He put his dustpan on the seat and got down behind the back of it, reaching out hesitantly with his fingers to touch the slime of the apple.

Or leave it, eh? Charlie wouldn't see it right down there.

'Get up inside, then, an' shut the door....'

Blast it! Too late! Oh well, show him, be on the same side with him as he got angry. That'd make a change. Ronnie levered himself up.

'Come on. . . .'

But the voice sounded a bit shaky for Charlie. And who was with him? Was he all right? Ronnie pushed himself hard against the back of the seat and looked down through the line of gaps—and in a sudden panicked drop he hit the floor again as if he'd been shot at, a noisy dive which was only masked by the angry slide and slam of the coach door.

'I told you not to come 'ere like this. Elsie don't like it, and. . . .'

'Belt up, Charlie!'

The unshaven voice made it unmistakably Roy Bradshaw, scowling as Ronnie had glimpsed him, his hard expression unmellowed by the five years it had been since that day when Ronnie had hidden behind the greasy cooker.

The blood pounded in Ronnie's ears. Scared rigid, head down, his ear-drums thumped an instinctive warning not to move. Breathing had suddenly become hard, and short shallow pants like an exhausted dog heightened his own shaky tenseness. Roy Bradshaw was Roy Bradshaw, and whatever he'd come here for it wouldn't be good. He'd only shake your hand if it was already right up your back. How the hell could he have ever thought this animal and his brother wouldn't do for him one day? Nervously swallowing the saliva which had collected from nowhere, Ronnie hunched down even smaller. He'd be stupid to show himself to the two of them now, he thought: because Christ knew where he stood. No, best to keep down out of the way till he'd sussed a few things out. Like, if Roy was here to sort Charlie out for taking him in, then he didn't want any part of it. But if Bernie had sent him from Val, to get him back because she was sorry, well, that'd be a bit different, wouldn't it? Or would it? Hell, he didn't know. So he'd hang on till he was sure. Find out. And not move a muscle meanwhile. . . .

'Now. . . .'

Ronnie heard Roy sit down on a seat, hard and firm, and

114

his boots scrape up on the fascia.

'... The French trip. I've got it all buttoned up now, all bar looking at this coach, which is why I've come out here while it's quiet, since you don't run to a nice private gar-ridge....'

Charlie said nothing, but Ronnie heard him light a cigar-ette with his clunky lighter, and he imagined his stubbly old face staring at Roy.

'Now, listen, like I said, the old-age people are straight, good as gold, and they're over the moon about going to Paris. And the stupid vicar can't do enough for us. Now that's important, because them not being bent's gonna do us the world of good. It's the start-off to something really big, this, so it's gotta be perfect. Get me? Perfect. Because word 'as it they're bloody queuing up over India to get in 'ere, an' if we get these three in like we ought to do—like we will, Charlie—we can ask what we want for anyone after. Sprat to catch a mackerel, see?' He dropped his voice, and Ronnie pictured him looking out of the coach window like some caged wolf before going on, very confidentially. 'With fron-tiers as long as they've got, France is wide open, the big back door, and we can 'ave all the big 'uns, the blokes the law's kicked out, or won't let near, adding noughts to the price just for the chance of being brought through it....'

Ronnie could almost hear him dribbling at the thought of all that money.

'Yeah, but....'

'No buts, Charlie. And stop worrying for Crissake! Once we're back 'ome the partition comes out an' no one knows it was ever there: it's only a bit of shaped hardboard. An' the bunks behind it come to pieces quicker than a kid's Meccano....'

'An' who's fixing that? Because I ain't in a position to....'

Roy bit him off. 'We'll come down an' fit it the night before. The fourteenth. Don't panic, Charlie. Now, all I want tonight are the measurements in the back. Yeah, and to tell you your date.' Ronnie heard the rustle of a scrap of paper. 'Depart Friday morning, 15th May, six a.m. Arrive back 'ere about eleven o'clock on the Sunday night.'

'Eh? Let 'em out 'ere?' Charlie coughed on his cigarette.

'Got to. The vicar and the old people mustn't know. So they go in Sunday afternoon at this place outside Boulogne, then get out here in the dark Sunday night. . . . '

'They'll bloody suffocate.' Charlie coughed again. 'Three of 'em.'

'No, we'll drill a few 'oles. They'll be all right. . . . '

'I dunno,' Charlie said in a low voice. 'It's all a bit chancy. I've said all along. I'm getting too old for all this, Roy. Besides, they'll be up to all this down the Customs. Bound to be. They'll go over this coach with a fine tooth comb. . . . '

Roy tried to sound patient, but it wasn't his style. 'You didn't listen, did you, Charlie? I told you before. When the old-age people get out to get their passports seen, all right, perhaps the Customs blokes'll have a dip down the backs of the seats. Perhaps. But that's different from the Immigration people, ain't it? Customs are looking for *things*: Immigration are looking for *people*. And you mark my words, with our crowd, all old and shaky after a dirty weekend in Paris, they ain't gonna waste their precious time on us. No one'll go near the back, you see if I ain't right. An' you're forgettin', Charlie, this partition's gonna be a real good job. . . . Now come on, stop wastin' my time; I wanna see the back. I ain't got long as it goes. . . . '

Ronnie heard Roy Bradshaw scrape off the fascia and stand up, and he screwed his eyes shut tight and nearly turned himself inside out in his effort to make himself smaller. God Almighty! This was too much! A real big-time racket! Just knowing about this was a killer! A death sentence! A big new racket like this, bringing in Indians in the backs of coaches, it was something you didn't have to know about if you wanted to stay alive.

And Ronnie did. Shaking there like a trapped rabbit, he very much wanted to stay alive.

And now they were coming up to see the back! He could hear the metallic flick of a steel rule. With his back to the gangway, vulnerable, unable even to see them as they got up to him, he suddenly wanted to stand up and scream and shout and bash and bite his way past them to the door. Except he wouldn't make it, he knew—not even with the kitchen knife which wasn't down his sock any more! The knife Charlie must have got the night he undressed him. Oh God! Christ! Mum! How the hell was he going to get out of this?

Braced for the first angry oath and the cut of the steel rule across his back he held his breath and listened ... and then, almost unbelievingly, he heard the slide of the coach door and the sound of boots on the metal steps. They were getting out, going round the side of the coach, past his window. The dog was up and barking: and Charlie, in a new, cruel voice cursed it.

Thank God for that! But what the hell did you do about all this?

The back of the coach, the big boot, opened with a dull thud, and then Ronnie suddenly knew where the Indians were going. And now he knew where he was going, too. Out of it, as fast as he could.

He snaked down the centre gangway like a commando; then, still doubled, he crawled down to the bottom step by the door and looked cautiously out. Judging by the slight see-saw movement down the coach's length the two of them were up in the boot, doing their measuring. Taking in a sharp, deep breath, as if he were suddenly going under water, Ronnie dived off the step and ran, doubled over, for the gate.

The dog went mad. Its front paws rose nearly a metre off the ground as the tight rope and the forward thrust lifted it up to bay its warning.

'What the 'ell . . . ?' roared Charlie from inside the boot.

But by the time he had clambered out the dog had settled to an angry bark at the gap in the gate, and the boy had gone.

10

Ronnie ran and didn't stop till he passed someone walking a calm dog along the sewer-bank. Then he lifted his head. Thank God! There were people about now, and nothing could happen in front of them, could it? Not that he'd been followed, or even been seen go; he was sure of that. And dogs couldn't talk yet, thank Christ. So, look normal quick, before someone else stuck their nose in, he told himself.

He slid down the bank's edge and did his best to look relaxed, plucking at stained grass, half-closing his eyes against the industrial sun; while inside him his heart was still thumping, his brain reeling with the painful shock of what he'd heard.

Charlie *was* mixed up with the Bradshaws, then; always had been from the sounds of it, and always would. Good job he hadn't been fooled by him, then. Good job he'd been a bit careful, held back from trusting him. You definitely couldn't trust anyone who was in with that mob. Good job he'd made his mind up from the start to clear off from Charlie Whitelaw's any time it suited him. He sat up. And good job he'd still got the key to the flat round his neck. They'd never touched that. Yeah! He could probably get his head down over the flat tonight and do a proper bunk tomorrow. Nick something, sell it, and get right out of this place. Go down the country somewhere out of all their rotten ways.... He rubbed his nose violently. Yeah, good job he could do that.

And he'd have to, by God, because when they found he'd gone from Charlie's they'd know he'd twigged. And then they'd want to find him real bad, being as how what he'd just found out could send all their plans up the spout for good. Roy and Bernie Bradshaw definitely wouldn't want their big racket kiboshed by him!

Ronnie shivered. Christ Almighty, he was in it now! He sat up and held his stomach as if he had a pain, and he rocked himself to and fro on the bank. He was all alone now, on his own and scared like he'd never been before—not even when he was little. Then he'd been scared of what they'd do if his dad got drunk and said something. Now there wasn't any 'if' about it. Now they just wanted him. And when they got him they'd do worse than hurt him. They'd kill him, wouldn't they? Because they did: they killed people who mucked up their big plans. People went missing all the time in all that new concrete....

Ronnie was trembling now, and his nose ran into his mouth. There was no one who could help him, no one he could trust: there was no one someone like him could ever trust, not even the law....

Then Ronnie suddenly cuffed his nose and stiffened. God, yes! The law! Kingsland. He could help him! Ronnie scrambled to his feet. Anything he could do to help, he'd said; for him or Steve; *anything he could do to help.* And he'd meant it like a kind of offer, hadn't he? A deal. The word about the football raid in exchange for letting Steve out quick. A copper's swap. Well, this was it, wasn't it? This was the time if ever there was one. This was when he *had* to do it, just to save his skin. All the guff on City East and the Indian smuggling would get Steve out, without any bother —and at the same time it'd make bloody sure the Bradshaws got put in....

The remembered offer calmed him a bit, and the hot

trembling stopped.

Yeah! That was what he'd do. Well, it had to be like that now because there was nothing to lose, nothing else he could do. Then him and his dad could get away out of it, for good. Yeah. A long way; a bloody long way. Perhaps over France. Or how about India? That sounded a good long way off. . . .

But when it came to it, it wasn't so easy: because there was no way Ronnie Webster could force himself up those steep steps and in under that blue light. The sight of it turned him over, and the thought of the enemy sitting inside with their distrusting scowls all ready to frown down at him made him feel sicker still. He wasn't telling nothing to them, that was for sure: but then he wouldn't get through to see Kingsland without.

What the hell to do? Ronnie clenched his fists and kicked a hard toe-cap at the wall in frustration. It was life and death whether or not he saw the man—and now he couldn't because he definitely wasn't going in here, and he didn't know where the copper lived to get to him there. He skulked in a shop doorway while he tried to think, frowning, thumping his thighs with the clenched fists, and trying to lose himself among the black plastic of Friday's refuse whenever anyone walked past. He leapt back furthest when he saw a minibus of traffic wardens: and then he suddenly had it. As he craned out to see where they were going he saw the winking lights indicating a left, hard left into the station yard. Yeah! No bother, that was it! That was the way round.

He let an eddying group from a bus suck him out of his doorway and carry him along the pavement past the station steps: and when he reached the wide entrance to the yard he drifted unnoticed inside. From where he was he could see some of the parked vehicles, the minibus emptying, the sleek, ready Rovers. But there was only one vehicle he wanted to see: Kingsland's grey Ford. Then at least he'd know if he was in with a chance. His face screwed with tension. He willed it to be there.

Silently among the High Street's traffic roar he inched further and further through the gate and along the wall by the side of the building, a step at a time, everything going quieter and quieter as he got further in. The pulse pounded louder in his head and his legs felt weak, but, pushed on now by the impetus of his own fear he reached the inner corner of the building and peered round and—oh, God! His muscles knotted up inside him as he suddenly saw the big black Daimler again, the motor Steve had driven that day to City East, the car with the card. Christ Almighty! A lifetime had passed since he'd sat up in the front of that horrible thing!

'No luck, Ronnie, you can't drive our evidence away!'

It was Kingsland and Jones walking in the quick way through the yard. Ronnie shot round and saw their friendly smiles, and their wide, blocking bodies. His first surprised instinct was to run. But there was no running past them. No backing out. And anyway, he sniffed, as he calmed a bit, this was what he'd come for, wasn't it?

'I wanna see you. . . .'

There was no more banter.

'O.K., son.'

The two men led Ronnie up the direct and secret route of back stairs and passages to the C.I.D. department. And then, alone with Kingsland in his inner office, Ronnie let the secret of the Bradshaws burst out with a sudden surging relief. It didn't take long because it wasn't a statement. It was short and jumbled, like an apology is, and it took several questions for Kingsland to get things clear in his mind. And if the detective was keeping his surprise at Ronnie's coming very much to himself, he certainly wasn't short on gratitude.

'Oh, that's terrific, Ronnie. Terrific.' He thumped the desk and made the 'phone jump. 'We've caught the odd one or two, the small stuff, and we knew the big boys were going to get in, somehow.' He fluffed his peak of thinning hair vigorously. 'But this is great—just the sort of information we wanted badly....'

But Ronnie wasn't jubilant. He sat on the chair and frowned at the policeman. He hadn't come here to help him; he'd come to help himself, and his dad. All he wanted next was for that 'phone to be picked up and word sent out for the Bradshaws and Charlie Whitelaw to be picked up. That was the deal, wasn't it? Not all this jumping up and down.

He cleared his throat, and sniffed, and put a clenched fist on the desk, near the telephone.

'Yes, I know. You want your dad out, don't you? And the others in. Yes, well so do I: but much as I want it, Ronnie, I'm afraid we can't even search them without evidence; not without either catching them at it, or getting someone in it to talk....'

Ronnie's eyes widened in surprise, and then he screwed them tight with disgust. What was all this? *He'd* talked, hadn't he? What was wrong with what he'd said? And where did this leave him? As if he didn't know. Out in the bloody cold, with the Bradshaws, didn't it?

'No, this is great. We'll pass this on to the Immigration Squad. Then they've got the whole set-up, and they can catch them red-handed, back here, as they arrive on English soil.' His face suddenly changed to lose the pleased smile, like a parent who has only just realized a child's disappointment in the cancellation of promised plans. 'But up to then it's no crime, you see, Ronnie, not while it's only in their minds. We *can't* touch 'em yet. In fact we daren't move too soon or we'll frighten them off.' His eyes lit up again and he playfully punched Ronnie's shoulder, now the big uncle pretending bad news was good. 'This'll do it, though, this'll do it. You've put us right on. And after that I'll pull all the strings I can with the legal people, tell them about your help, and see what we can do. Leave that to me, Ronnie. I won't let you down....'

Kingsland stood up, one part of him clearly wanting to get going, to tell his guv'nor about their good fortune, but another part of him very aware now of the boy's sense of defeat in coming to him at all.

'And don't you worry.' The boy's face was no longer animated; it was tight, independent, the eyes reflecting only a look of abandonment, of mistrust. 'We've known where you were, Ronnie. We haven't let you go. One false move and we'll have you out of there in no time, don't worry....'

Leave it out! If one false move was a knife in the guts there was nothing they *could* do about it! And what was he saying? Go back there? Go back to what he'd just run away from?

Kingsland sat on his desk with his hands in his lap. Excited as he was, this needed patient handling. 'Listen, Ronnie. You said they didn't see you, didn't you? Now, if you go back straight away, quickly—you can tell them ... say that dog frightened you and you ran off—Charlie and Elsie Whitelaw won't bother you, I know. Not if they've been treating you like Prince Ronnie so far. That's not their scene. And Bradshaw won't still be there. Anyway, I'll have you under observation. But going back'll keep it all looking normal, don't you see?—and that's important. Whereas,' he rubbed his nose vigorously, 'if you clear off they'll know you've twigged, and we'll be wasting all our time trying to catch them in the act....'

Ronnie sniffed and ran his nose down his arm. He wasn't anything like so sure as this bloke. It was all very nice to sound certain about things up here, with all these coppers to protect you—especially when you weren't the one in it yourself. No, it all depended where you stood. They all had their special angle, didn't they?

'It's definitely the best way, Ronnie. This way we stand a chance of getting shot of the Bradshaws for good: get 'em off all our backs, permanently....'

Ronnie opened one eye a bit wider and looked at the

policeman's serious face. Was he having him on? He sniffed again. How come there were so many grown-ups who looked at you straight like that, and nodded like that, when they were telling you what was best for you—but not for them?

Why the hell couldn't there be a world without them?

'We'll give you a lift part of the way back: then you'll have to walk the rest.... But this is the best way, Ronnie, believe me....'

The man moved, and Ronnie's huge sigh summed up all that was unfair in the whole set-up, everything rotten in the whole stinking world. Then he grunted, a short-hand sound to stand for all the frustrated words he wanted to say but couldn't, and he followed the detective out, faced-about again.

And as he passed through the outer office of the C.I.D. room D.C. Jones stood away from the door quickly, and secretly put his thumbs up.

'Well done, guv,' he said quietly. 'I knew it'd pay off.'

D.I. Kingsland didn't reply. Because, like Ronnie, he'd never really expected to be understood.

Going back to 'The Farm' took all the guts Ronnie could grip hold of. Charlie was the enemy now, the real, shown-up enemy, and here Ronnie was walking into the enemy camp without any protection that he could see—just Kingsland's shaky word that he was being watched. It was a gamble, win all or lose all, and it was Ronnie who was the one who stood to gain—or lose—most. His throat felt swollen and his bowels rolled with apprehension as he reluctantly pushed a gap in the gate, and his skin seemed to suddenly freeze over when the alsation, already aroused by his going, rose to a fever of warning on the first sign of his return.

Charlie must have been tense, too, because he appeared in the doorway instantly, scowling at the intrusion and somehow looking bigger than he had for a couple of days.

124

Ronnie tried to swallow, to call something out: but he couldn't. He was trembling now. Christ, he shouldn't have done this! This was the worst move he could ever have made. Bloody Kingsland! So: turn and run? Or what?

'Oh, it's only you, Ronnie. 'Ello, son. Where you been?' He didn't sound menacing. And instead of walking towards Ronnie, to grab him, he turned back into the house, smacking the dog's nose on the way. 'Shut up you! It's only Ronnie!'

Oh, God! What now, then? Was the copper right after all? Because it suddenly looked as if he might be, didn't it? Feeling a bit more confident Ronnie went cautiously over to the man and the unconvinced dog. But one false move and he'd turn and shoot off like a chased hare.

''E put the wind up me,' he said, ''ad a go at me, so I ran out the gate. Then I lost myself over the marshes.'

'You be'ave yourself, Bruce!' Charlie said, smacking the dog's rump this time. 'This is Ronnie. 'E lives 'ere, get it? We can bloody do without you playing up. . . .'

So as Bruce laid himself down carefully like a Sphinx on hot sand Ronnie went cautiously indoors: where, in spite of a quietness about the place—which could have been in Ronnie's imagination—everything seemed to be the same as it had been before.

After a while, when Charlie went into his office and Elsie was steaming up the kitchen, Ronnie said he was going outside to the dog. ''E don't know me proper, yet,' he told the knot in Elsie's apron. He stood in the doorway and called 'Bruce'; but the animal was content to sit and look at him, an uncertain stare, and Ronnie quickly took his chance to go back to the coach and get on with cleaning it. He could cover his tracks that way, he thought, so they wouldn't know he'd been in the coach earlier on.

But he needn't have bothered, as it turned out. Charlie spent the rest of the evening shut away in his office, and there was no further sign of the Bradshaws. Only Elsie paid

Ronnie much heed, but it was bacon and clean pyjamas that seemed to worry her rather than Ronnie's loyalties. And when he went to bed Ronnie felt relieved, because it seemed as if Kingsland had been right, and yet he was strangely apprehensive, because in his experience things always seemed to go quiet just before something happened to throw his world into chaos.

The closed doors along Ronnie's landing shut off several secret worlds. He'd never been inside any of them, although he knew the one next to the bathroom was Charlie's. In the few days he'd been there he'd never found out what lay behind the others: and especially whether Elsie slept in one of them or not. In spite of the 'grandad' and 'nan' stuff, she could have been Charlie's sister, or a cousin, or just kept house for him with a bedroom to herself, for all he knew. It had nagged at Ronnie, mildly. That night, though, he found out.

He couldn't sleep; and the more he tried the further away sleep went; it was like trying to put his arms round a wreath of mist. His legs shot about the bed, and he turned and returned his pillow. He could have taken two sleeping tablets and still he wouldn't have slept: the computer in his brain wouldn't switch off: defensive, protecting him, it wouldn't let him rest while there was still some sorting out, some satisfying, to do.

He thought he'd fooled them; he thought he hadn't been found out, that he was safe. But was he? Were they putting on an act for him? What did they really know? What were they really going to do?

His door didn't lock, did it? So he wouldn't stand much chance if they came in the night. It was all right for Kingsland to talk. His men were supposed to be keeping an eye on him. But they weren't in here: they weren't under the bloody bed, were they?

He had to know what they were up to, Charlie and Elsie.

He couldn't sleep with the thought of one of them coming in in the night, like one of them had when they'd undressed him. He had to put his mind that much at rest, to know whether he'd fooled them enough to keep them at bay for the night. And that could mean only one thing; he had to have a listen; see if they were asleep, or if they were awake, planning something.

Well, that wouldn't be too hard. He'd creep out on the landing, listen at a couple of doors, and decide what to do from there—and if they found out, well, he could always pretend he was on his way to the lav.

Quietly, and yet trying to look businesslike, in case he was surprised, Ronnie opened his bedroom door and slowly made his way along the landing. No sound. All he could hear were his feet on the runner and the noise of his own halted breathing. Nothing. The house was dead quiet. Even the woodwork had settled and was silent. It definitely didn't sound as if anyone was plotting to get him.

So he went to the lavatory.

And it was while he was standing there, alone in that special private quietness which goes with hair curlers and whispers after the lights have been put out, that he heard them: Charlie and Elsie in the room next door. But this was no whispered conspiracy. What he heard was no controlled, planning voice. This was high, and whining, not unlike the dog when it was upset: and it was crying. It was Charlie Whitelaw. As soon as he heard it Ronnie wanted urgently to be safely back in his bed and deep beneath the covers, because this had nothing to do with his safety; did it? He had no business hearing this. Overhearing Roy Bradshaw had been dangerous. But this was something else, this crying. This was *private*, and Ronnie wanted to learn nothing here.

Standing as still as he could he waited for a louder cry, both of them going at once like in an argument, so that he could scuttle back to his room. It usually happened sooner or later. But the hoped-for crescendo didn't come, and Ronnie was trapped there, listening to their misery.

'... Oh God, what a ... bloody ... rotten world!' Charlie's quivering voice was high and unsure, and Ronnie could hear the muffle of him punching a pillow, practically see the dribble running down the man's chin. ''E says ... "jump" ... an' we all bloody jump. 'E's got the 'ole of the ... East End ... doin' what 'e says. We're all ... bloody ... trapped....'

'Sssssh, Charlie, ssssssh,' said Elsie. 'You'll find a way out....'

'No. No, I won't.' He moaned again, like a big animal in pain, a creature that was powerless to help itself. 'One mistake, turning that lorry of 'is over ... an' I get six months in hospital with a broken back ... an' the rest of my life to pay my dues. "Do this bloody job ... do that" .... An' I'm hooked. I'm in, and there'll never be no "out" because there never bloody is.... It's all force and violence ... the law of the jungle ... grovelling to the strongest....' His voice ran on, dull and painful, like blood from an open wound.

'Oh, ssssh....'

'You ain't allowed to make a go of anything round 'ere. Not a couple of coaches; not even takin' on young Ronnie.' He cried again, louder this time, his voice trembling in his throat. 'We've never been so normal 'ere till just recent ... an' now it's all gonna go, Els; with all this new business it's all gonna go....'

'No it ain't, Charlie. Sssssh....'

There was a long pause, and some muffled sobbing; and then the high grizzle of Elsie's own unhappiness eventually joined in. And while they tried to keep their comforting quiet, Ronnie shifted his weight, slid the bolt, and ghosted back to his bedroom.

Oh, God! What sort of a turn-up was this? The warm darkness beneath his own covers wrapped him round with a new security. So Charlie was all right after all! Charlie *wasn't* bent. He was just the same as a lot of others, trying to live ordinary, but forced and threatened by the Bradshaws. Just like Steve. Frightened by the brothers like Ronnie was himself. He suddenly stiffened, his toes curling. Yeah! Charlie was a bit like him, wasn't he? He could see it now. So the Bradshaws hadn't broken the driver's back like the kids' story went, but they'd got him where they wanted him, living his life with his neck twisted around looking for trouble, just like Ronnie. He was lying there crying in the other room because they'd ruined his life for him; just like they had for Ronnie.

Ronnie turned and faced the other way. And something else had lumped him up in that bathroom, another thing, a sort of jealous feeling he'd never really had before, not quite like that. It was her. Elsie. And him. Them being together, comforting, crying next to one another; the big man and the little woman. That was something new, different, and, well ... nothing like Steve and Val. They were never like that. Val only ever wanted for herself. And God knew what Steve wanted. You wouldn't have heard *them* crying in bed together. One of them would've been knocking back a drink, and the other one would've been spraying her hair to go out somewhere, you could bet on that.

No, mate, Ronnie suddenly thought, if this was being near to normal, here at Charlie's, then to be honest he liked it: good grub, regular; a little job for spending money; someone talking to you now and again; it was quite good, as far as anything *could* be good for someone in his fix.

And he'd just been all the way up to the nick to tell Kingsland how to ruin it!

It wasn't his fault; of course it wasn't, he knew that: no one could say it was. But whose fault it was didn't come into it. He'd ruined it, that was what counted.

Ronnie felt choked. His eyes began to fill, and his nose ran. Yeah, thrown it away, hadn't he? At the same time as he'd landed Charlie in a mess which he could never clear up.

He turned over again. He'd never thought much of his own chances of doing anything. Not *anything*. And now his chances were smaller than ever, he thought, as the memory of Charlie's sobbing in the room across the landing sounded loud in his head.

11

Charlie and Elsie seemed like different people to Ronnie over breakfast the next morning. It was like meeting someone he'd only ever seen at a distance: like hearing their voice for the first time, or seeing them from a different close-up angle: he seemed to be getting a new picture of them, and it was hard to grasp how he'd ever seen them any other way. What Charlie said and what Elsie did could only be taken one way now; open and above board; there was nothing scary underneath. Ronnie, from having taken a chance on them in the first place, all suspicious and wary, then having been dead scared the night before, now felt he was definitely with them; relaxed and a lot more trusting than he had ever been before. It was a new feeling for him, and like with a new pair of trousers, he wasn't sure how it suited him, until, pottering in the yard that Saturday morning he caught sight of his face in a wing mirror. At first it gave him a mild shock; it seemed like someone else—him, but someone else—and he wasn't sure why. Then he realized. He'd caught himself smiling; just a little bit in spite of himself; and he'd had to wipe it off to check.

Who'd have thought Charlie was the coach driver who'd

scared him? The man with the sewn-up back who made you sit up in the coach? The dangerous crook who wanted to be in it up to his neck with the Bradshaws? This man smiled, and winked, and made 'Ronnie' sound like a new name when it was said in his deep, throaty voice.

'Ronnie, mate, tell Elsie to put a kettle on. I'm off out with this bus at one, tell her....'

And it seemed a bit like that all day; a feeling of being where he felt he ought to be, of belonging there. But it was a fierce unspoken belonging, the sort he'd seen people have in funerals in the flats: old ladies for dead old men, a dad once for a dead baby: because rolling round inside his belly like a hot ball bearing was an intense feeling that it was over already: that this was something he'd already killed off for himself.

Manjit Kaur sat next to her mother on the carpeted floor of the Gurdwara, listening to an old man reading from the scripture beneath the canopy, his voice lost for seconds at a time as heavy buses stopped with a regular squeak outside, and then roared off again. Her attention wandered and she felt bad, the only one not listening intently. But as she stared about her she thought she saw more clearly the way things were, and she knew she wasn't really wickedly wasting her time.

She saw the bright festoons suspended above their heads in a false, glittering, ceiling; and beyond them the cement walls and girders of the old warehouse. She saw the musicians, so important to their meeting, straight-backed and skilled; yet tomorrow they would be the dustman and the old man with watery eyes who sat on the front coping. And she saw the men across the aisle on the right, the young ones as strictly turbanned as the old, in their Co-op shirts and High Street cords. And she saw more clearly than ever how her life was taking place within another life, and of the separateness of it. But her eyes stayed longest on Sarinder, her brother, sitting nearer the fathers now than the young men, his eyes serious and responsible: and seeing him trying so hard made her long even more for her father's return. For this loss, she thought, was a separateness which need not be: and she made up her mind that lawfully or unlawfully she desperately wanted her father to be here, now, sharing this meeting, giving his strength to them all.

Sarinder had explained it to her, and she had understood. Her father hadn't done any wrong in the strict sense. He had tried to help a relative with money, a cousin for whom he was responsible as the head of the family; and in getting the money he had run a risk, and had lost, and had been left outside. Now it was only the law he was breaking, a law which sometimes changed with changes of men, and he was doing no wrong to any man, or to God. So whether it was through the airport lounge that he came, walking, or in a coach, cramped up in some secret part, he was not a different person. He was still her gentle father.

Needing to break the law was just one more separateness which some people had to live with, Manjit decided.

There wasn't much Ronnie could do about anything now. He could feel bad about things, but feeling bad didn't make any difference to what happened, so he just went where he had to and carried on till something stopped him, the same as always.

Life went on at school as it always had, and Ronnie got through Monday as he always had, all deaf ears and frown-tightened eyes.

It was after school when something stopped Ronnie. And as usual, it hadn't taken long to happen. He was scuffing to the gate, hands in his pockets, his mind nowhere in particular, when he was suddenly aware of being watched, that odd feeling that he sometimes felt, that was like a slight tap on the shoulder. He looked up, and his stomach squeezed. Oh God, no! It had happened at last. It was Bernie

Bradshaw, sitting in his long car on the 'No Waiting' lines. The old terror twisted inside Ronnie like a cold blade. Bradshaw! They did know, then; and this one was waiting for him. The man with the unblinking eyes which screwed up on sight of him and said, 'You! It's you I'm after!'

Christ! Ronnie's dry mouth fell open and he flicked his eyes to left and right. Who else was there? Was it just Bradshaw in the car, or were there others about? Then Ronnie saw the big man starting to get out. No, he was on his own, but he was definitely coming for him. God, what did he do, where did he go without just giving up and looking guilty as hell by running away? He looked round behind him towards the school: what about back inside to get something? Hell, he didn't know. That'd look all wrong, wouldn't it?

He stood there rooted in a dither of panic, until Manjit Kaur suddenly came running swiftly out of the building, arms straight by her sides. Yeah! That was it! Thank God! She always ran off like the devil was after her. That was a chance, because without looking like he was running away from Bradshaw, now Ronnie could still race off out of it.

''Ere you, I wan' you!' he shouted as she went past—but not so forcefully that she should stop—and, pretending not to have seen Bernie Bradshaw, he jerked and threaded through a waist-high muddle of little kids after the Indian girl.

On to him wasn't he? Ronnie told himself as he ran. So some bent copper had dropped him in it! Told Bradshaw about him hearing all that stuff on the coach. There were plenty who took back-handers, he knew that.

Ronnie ran hard to keep pace with the girl, and his transparent skin filled with the deep red of effort. But he'd be all right, he thought, for a street or two. Good job he was used to running. It'd take Bradshaw a bit of time to turn his big car round, and by then he'd have lost him in some of his old back-doubles. And running, doing something about it, definitely took the edge off being scared for a bit: but he'd feel sick again when he stopped, he knew that, thinking what Bradshaw was going to do to him, how he'd hurt him. . . .

But Ronnie was not the only one with a racing mind, and Manjit knew full well when she was being chased. Before she crossed the busy High Street she looked round again, and she saw the strange boy still coming after her. She saw his tight face with the staring eyes and the streaming hair, looking like some angry demon, and she panicked, too. What had she done against him now? Would he just kick her again for no reason? She turned and ran out into the road, halting a juggernaut with a hiss and a stream of abuse, and, clutching up her tunic for easier movement, she sped for home along the crowded street.

Behind them both Bernie Bradshaw, frowning slightly, negotiated the busy junction with the ease the driver of an expensive car expects. Chewing, with white teeth exposed, he took a half-corona cigar from a box beside him and lit it from the dashboard: then he picked out the small figure of the boy zigzagging on the pavement and gave himself just enough speed to keep him in view.

Up the road Manjit heard a woman curse somewhere behind her.

'Little swine, you! Look where you're going, can't you?'

'Get stuffed!'

The girl looked round. It was Ronnie, colliding with a shopper. He was closer now, his face twisted with dislike at the woman and with a new frown of determination. He was coming up fast. If he wanted to speak to her why didn't he call her name? Running after her like that could mean there was only harm for her, she was sure. She tried to run faster, and panic widened her brown eyes. Games of chase in the park, when her father had allowed her to run, had been very different to this. At the end of this she was going to be hurt, she knew that. But the emergency seemed to give her some of the extra speed she wanted, and she twisted, leaned, checked and spurted, racing along through the people, brushing and bumping, parting a pair of pensioners, and halting a pregnant woman to a shriek of complaint.

Ronnie came after her, taking the gutter as a fast lane when he lost sight of her among the bodies and bags, and behind them both Bernie Bradshaw had to increase the pressure on his accelerator. But in overtaking a bus he came up close, and Ronnie, darting a look at the traffic, saw him again, frowning, well within reach, and he thought he'd never get the next breath in.

God, this *was* real this time! Bradshaw was there, after him: no frightening dream, this. He put his head down and the old skill came, the imagined runs from six years up paid off, and he did now what he'd done all those times before. He suddenly turned on himself without stopping, shot back across the pavement, and raced off down a side road, throat burning, blood in the mouth, the final all-out effort. Running full tilt he turned his head to check. Had it worked? God, yes! Bradshaw had overshot. Must have. No sign of him. Just time to hide. Get down behind a coping before the Rover made it. He looked at the grey houses to choose one. Vital, this was! Quick! Quick! One with no gate, a bit run-down, where no old bag'd come out and tell him to clear off out of her front garden. No kids, neither. Quick!

Then he saw her at the door. And she saw him. Manjit. Trembling, fumbling with a key. Shocked she was, about to scream. Only one thing for it! He ran into the porch, threw a grimy hand round her mouth, and against her violent struggles, kicking, knee-ing, biting, he took over the key, turned it, and pushed her sprawling through the door where they landed, knee'd and elbowed, on the hard hallway lino.

'No! Help me!'

'Shut your face!' he hissed, finding her mouth again with his hand, his eyes darting at the inside doors for warning of someone charging out of a room, his feet finding the front door and slamming it with a violent kick.

135

'They're after me! Gonna kill me!' He clambered astride her like a street bully, thrust his face close to hers, and staring truth into her eyes he repeated it slowly between indrawn breaths. 'They're ... gonna ... kill me!' He let the worst of the pressure off his clamping hand and he kept staring; and she didn't scream or struggle any more. 'You savvy? Kill!' He drew his hand across his throat in a gesture he knew she'd understand.

Her eyes were wide, but her mouth was shut, and she nodded.

Suddenly, he let her go and stood up. Trying the first door he looked cautiously into the room, and checking what he knew already by now—that the house was empty—he rushed to the netted window and looked out, up and down the street. No sign. The Rover wasn't there. He'd done it, then. He was all right for a bit. No one'd ever think to look for him here. He flopped down on the settee, elbows on knees, and dropped his head between his legs. He drew in a deep breath, pent it up, and blew it out noisily. Manjit came slowly round the door, still struggling for breath herself, and rubbing a smarting elbow.

This strange, spiteful boy, she thought. What were these devils that chased him all the time?

He looked up. The scared Paki. What was going on inside her funny head? She knew more about him than he knew about her. But she was safe as houses. Once she was over being scared, he was sure she was safe.

'I ain't lying,' he said at last. 'This bloke, big gang bloke, 'e's after me, and 'e ain't playin' about, either. 'E don't. If 'e thinks 'e's gonna do anything to you, 'e does it.' He looked towards the window again. 'An' 'e's after me....'

He was glad it was safe telling her, it was like he'd thought before, the same as talking to some pet who'd never tell; and besides, he desperately needed help while he laid low for a bit; just while he gave Bernie Bradshaw time to get fed up searching round the streets; while he decided what to do. He got up and checked the street again, careful not to touch the net. Still no sign.

'Why?'

'Eh?' He sat down again, and sniffed.

'Please, why will this man wish to hurt you?' She, too, checked the street; but not for Bradshaw; for her mother. She wasn't coming. Manjit sat down at the other end of the settee.

Good question, he thought. Bloody good question. He scowled; but he didn't bother to give the girl a reason. At the moment he was more concerned with what he was going to do about it all; how he could hang about till it was safe to get back to Charlie and tell him how they were both in the same cart: because that was going to be favourite now, he thought. Come out with it: all of it, except the bit about Kingsland knowing, of course. He daren't tell him that.

'What time does your mum and dad get in?' he asked. He pointed to the clock. 'How long ... before ... your mum and dad gets in?'

Manjit closed her eyes briefly. How long would it be before people outside her family spoke to her normally? 'My mother comes home soon; then my brother, from North East London College. But my father will not come home tonight. . . .'

Oh. So he'd better make a move soon, Ronnie thought, before he got involved with her old lady. He nodded, and sniffed, and turned his head towards the window.

Manjit frowned. Didn't the boy want to know about her father? she thought. Not *all* about him; but about him being absent from the home, like *his* mother was? There were more children than this boy who had reason to be unhappy.

'My father is in India,' she said. 'But he is coming to Europe soon. . . .'

'Oh, yeah,' he said. 'You writ it down. . . .' Ronnie pretended a surface millimetre of interest. Best to keep her

137

talking for a bit, because he still couldn't get away for a few minutes, not till he knew for certain that the Rover had cleared right off out of it. And he didn't want any more wrestling. 'I wouldn't mind going up in an aeroplane. . . .'

'That's the easy way,' Manjit snapped. 'My father has to come by land and sea. It is very hard. He has to come across countries to France, and then by sea to England. . . .'

Ronnie suddenly stiffened and stared at her. Do what? Did she say *France*? That didn't sound right. That wasn't how they all came over. Christ, that sounded more like what Roy Bradshaw had been on about, the back door, didn't it? France? The bent way? Oh, God! He screwed up his eyes, and sniffed. Was she part of all this, then? The Bradshaws and the Indian-smuggling? Had he run right into it? He opened his blue eyes wide and twisted his mouth un-naturally to ask, in a display of innocent interest, 'When's that, then? About a month off? In a coach, is it?'

Manjit stood up and the blood seemed to drain from her. Her legs went weak. Oh, no! Of course, the boy knew about it; the coach she'd seen: and it was all supposed to be so secret, that part of it. 'Perhaps,' she said. Oh, help me, someone, please. She looked at him, her eyes pleading; but all she wanted to do now was to cover her stupid mouth with her own hands. What complication had she made by being so determined to show him that she was suffering too?

'Yeah,' Ronnie said, for the sake of saying something. No doubt about it. They were both in it, then. But were they on the same side really, or opposite? Did this mean he could trust her now, or not?

He frowned, and he decided to trust only the natural reaction which came to him at times like this. Run. Get away out of it. Now he definitely didn't want her old lady to see him here, to recognize him, to be able to finger him when things went wrong for her. It was bad enough having the Bradshaws after him, without all the Indians. . . .

He got up and walked quickly to the street door. Opening it carefully, like a man with an alarm-wired safe, he checked the porch, the small cemented garden, the street—both the pavement and the road. All clear, he thought; no Bradshaw and no one black coming who could possibly be the girl's mother. He'd get back from this place to Charlie's double-quick.

'See you,' he said.

'Good-bye.' Her face was still very straight, and paler now.

Ronnie ran; and as he ran he went over what he'd say when he got in to Charlie's. All along the sewer bank, safe from cruising cars, he rehearsed as he ran: because he'd got a bomb to drop, he knew it: and it was going to be a big risk, seeing what Charlie did when he found out Ronnie knew everything. It was going to turn Charlie's plans upside down: and there was no way of ever knowing how people would take to things like that. Like Steve. When he'd been dropped in it—by Val, as it turned out—he'd turned something rotten, hadn't he? When people were scared or upset themselves they acted differently to when they weren't. Like Val herself. She'd been a lot like that, he thought. If he broke something it was a good shout when she was all right, and a kicking round the kitchen when she was in one of her moods. You never knew. You were always taking a chance, even with people like Charlie.

Even so, he'd got no real choice tonight. It was Hobson's for him, because with the Bradshaws on to him, Charlie was his only lifeline now. They needed Charlie, so Charlie could probably buy him some protection. He hoped. If he wanted to, that was. The police were useless, that was for sure, and he couldn't run away from the Bradshaws, no one could. But now that he knew the truth about Charlie he hoped like hell Charlie would sort it out—somehow.

The trouble was, he had to get in, tell Charlie, and get

him to get something going before they came. Because they would come, he knew that; too right they would, sooner or later.

Ronnie approached 'The Farm' from the other side of the road, keeping well down in the littered ditch which separated the waste land of tipped rubbish from the road. He knew the car he was looking for, the Rover which would keep him hiding in the ditch as long as it remained. But it wasn't there, unless it was inside the yard; and he was pretty sure neither of the Bradshaws would leave it further round the corner, and walk. He let a bus bounce past, and then he ran quickly across the road like a ferret, flattening himself against the gate to look through. No. It was all clear. There were just the two coaches in the yard, and the dog.

So this was it. Now to find out whether he was going to sleep here tonight, or rough it out somewhere.

Bruce had been getting quieter, a bit more used to him, he thought. The dog would still slide on his claws towards him, barking, but he stopped sooner these days; and Ronnie was thankful for that because tonight he didn't want there to be any more noise to carry news of his arrival than was necessary.

Ronnie started calling as soon as he had a hand through the gate. 'Brucie, boy; good boy; good Brucie.' He walked up to the animal, selling it on a soft welcome like a man taking a grenade away from a toddler. 'Good boy, good Bruce....'

Bruce exploded into sound.

'Sssssh, boy, sssssh.' Then he passed by him, closer than before, as the barking quickly subsided. He stopped at the back door and took a deep breath. Now.

In the kitchen Elsie was alone, reading Sunday's paper. She raised her eyebrows. 'Cup of tea?' she asked, getting up. 'Take one in to Charlie, eh? 'E's doing his books.'

'Yeah, O.K.' Well, that might be a bit easier, Ronnie thought, telling Charlie on his own without Elsie. It was going to be rotten anyway, but it might help a bit—having it out on their own first.

He stood waiting awkwardly by the table while the kettle went slowly through its changes of tune; but it wasn't fast enough for him, and he shrugged and sniffed at his next small plan going wrong as he heard a noise, sensing Charlie behind him in the doorway. He turned to see how his face looked today, to see how he'd take it.

But no! Oh, God! Ronnie's mouth dropped open. It wasn't Charlie. It was Bernie Bradshaw, filling the doorway with smart menace: and from behind him came a short shout: and then Charlie came in, pushed violently into the kitchen by a sweating, hard-faced Roy.

A sharp-nailed, invisible hand thrust into Ronnie's guts with the real, twisting pain of terror. This was it again. The feeling he'd had in his own kitchen when he was little. There was nothing on God's earth like this real terror of imminent violence: here, now, within seconds. Ronnie fought to hold his stomach in, and his bowels, but even as the nauseous waves shocked through him, his other instincts—self-survival, retreat from danger—were shocked into action too. The back door? There wasn't one out of here, and the window was only open a crack. Through their legs? No chance! Men like these were up to all the tricks. Ronnie's chest was tight, like an engine seizing up, and he gasped for air. It was like in nightmares when you had no breath for making a voice. He felt weak, faint, and the room began to swim....

''Ere, what the 'ell's going on?' Charlie demanded, rounding on Roy and shrugging the hard grip off his shoulder. Man to man, in his own house, he'd fight if he had to.

'You bloody know....'

'Like 'ell I do! What you playing at, springing in 'ere and pushing me about?' He suddenly looked round towards the door through which the brothers had made their silent entrance. 'An' the dog...?'

Bernie, leaving the physical stuff to Roy, sat down in Elsie's small armchair and hitched his sharp, fawn trousers. ''E's 'aving a little sleep, Charlie. While we 'ave our chat. Only it's very important we don't 'ave no distractions while we sort a few things out. . . . '

Elsie stood tense and silent at the sink, her lips a grim line, her experienced East End eyes on Charlie. Ronnie, too, getting a better grip on himself now the talking had started, was staring at the big man. He knew what they were both thinking. This was the real thing going on, what everyone was scared of round here; a sorting out visit from both the Bradshaws.

'Sit down!' Roy pushed the bewildered Charlie into a chair at the table. Then he went back to stand at the kitchen door, which he closed with a kick.

They were trapped, like prisoners in a torture cell, Ronnie thought. He shivered. If only the dog had barked. Half-a-minute might have given them a chance.

Bernie Bradshaw nodded at a chair opposite Charlie, up at the table. 'You, over there,' he said to Ronnie. And Ronnie sat there facing Charlie's puzzled, frightened, stare. Bradshaw rose smoothly from his chair.

'You're a bloody idiot, Charlie, telling the kid. He's running through the streets, in and out of the girl's house, a sure sign for any nosy copper that there's something going on between this place and that. Or some grass. Anyone can put two and two together when the bloke suddenly comes 'ome from nowhere—and then it's straight round the nick for a quick dropsie. . . . '

'Eh?'

'The boy!' Bernie suddenly stabbed towards Ronnie with a cigar, close; and the boy looked wildly round, goose-pimpling at the thought of him using it for real.

'Christ, 'e don't know!' Charlie exploded. 'What you on about? I never told 'im nothing! What the 'ell d'you think I am?'

'I wouldn't like to say, Charlie.' Bernie looked at the glowing cigar end and squinted up into the cloud of smoke. 'But you tell me why the kid comes tearing out of school with the black girl and goes running straight round 'er 'ouse. This afternoon, when I was waiting outside to give 'im a fiver from 'is mother. . . .'

Charlie looked across at Ronnie again, pain and betrayal in his eyes. Is this how you thank us for taking you in? they seemed to say.

But that was only one of Ronnie's worries. Had he really led to all this for nothing, by running away? he wanted to know. Had Bradshaw really only come that afternoon to give him a fiver?

Bernie Bradshaw stood at the end of the table, suddenly thrusting his face forward to spit tobacco bits at the boy. 'You do bloody know, don't you?' He held his face there, staring his cold pale eyes at Ronnie, and Ronnie knew there'd be no lying.

He nodded. 'Yeah,' he muttered, turning his face away.

Bernie looked back at Charlie, and then at the boy again. 'An' 'ow did you know?' he asked, spelling it out for everyone before taking the next necessary action.

The answer came back with the speed of truth. 'I 'eard 'im,' he said, turning his head at Roy. 'I was in the coach, cleaning out, an' 'e came an' said it all to Charlie. . . .'

'What?' Roy's back came off the door as if it had been kicked open from outside. 'You bleedin' little liar!'

Charlie moved too, and was off his feet blocking Roy's way to Ronnie with a very broad shoulder. 'No, leave 'im!' he shouted. 'I'll make 'im right! 'E 'as been cleaning out for me, regular. That's more than possible, what 'e says.'

But Roy wasn't going to back down yet. His voice, high and nasal with anger, strained at Ronnie. 'All right, then, son, what did I say?'

Now they were all staring at Ronnie. This was important. This went to the root of who you could trust, and who had been less careful than he should have been.

'Yeah, come on, boy,' Charlie told him.

'Tell 'im!' Bernie ordered.

Ronnie sniffed; his hands were clenched by his sides, and he gave up looking at anyone, staring at the floor with his head averted as if he were back in front of Miss Neame, his voice as wavery as the cross of an illiterate signing a fateful document.

'Well, you just said you was gonna go over France ... in a coach ... an' bring back these ... you know, Indians ... in the back....'

'Yeah. How?' Roy's attacking question was like a physical move towards him.

'Be'ind a board or suthink. Be'ind the cases. Through the back door, you said....'

'Yeah.' Bernie sat down again and stared first at Roy and then at his cigar, which had gone out. 'And what about the girl?' he asked.

Ronnie's knuckles were clenched white. The strain was killing. He'd had enough. 'I just know 'er. She's in my school,' he shouted. 'I can't 'elp that, can I? An' I couldn't 'elp bloody 'earing!'

Bernie sat back and crossed his legs. 'All right,' he said. 'All right.' With an impatient wave of his flabby hand he told Roy to sit down away from the door. 'But the point is now, the point is, is anyone gonna put two an' two together, you an' her, when her old man comes 'ome?'

Ronnie, sensing a drop in the temperature, tried to lower it further. 'Well, we ain't friends. No one thinks that. I've give 'er a couple o' kicks, an' I knocked 'er down s'afternoon; so if anyone was watchin'....'

There was a long silence, and Ronnie sensed everyone working out the next move. The only trouble was, one way or another, he was going to be the counter.

Suddenly Bernie stood up. 'Roy an' me's gonna 'ave a little word outside,' he said. 'You 'ang on 'ere.' Then very nonchalantly he lit his cigar again and let Roy stand aside for him as he led the way out through the door.

The three who were left in the room looked at one another. Then, 'You should 'a told me,' said Charlie. 'I could 'a told you 'ow to go on about it. . . .'

Ronnie scowled, and Elsie said, 'We're not . . . you know . . .' She waved a brittle thin arm at where the Bradshaws were. The boy sniffed. He knew they weren't part of it of their own choosing, he'd heard it in the night, hadn't he? But that wasn't going to be much consolation if the Bradshaws were spinning up outside for who got rid of him. All he was now was a bloody nuisance to everyone, all round, he thought. For the lot of them he'd be better off out of the way, he could see that.

He looked at the door. He wished he'd taken more notice of how the land lay inside the house. He bet the Bradshaws had gone into Charlie's office opposite. But if he ran into the passage he couldn't turn right because that's where the dog was, knocked out, probably with one of the gang there ready to do it again. And he wasn't sure about left: past the living-room they were just doors which could have gone anywhere, to the outside or into cupboards: he'd never had cause to go through them, nor even to take in the evidence of the shoe-scuffs and scratches on them.

'Stay where you are,' Charlie said, curtly, reading his thoughts. 'No one's gonna 'urt you. They can't do much now. Things are too far gone to cut me out. There ain't time to change nothing. And they know they can only push me so far when it comes to bother for a kid like you. . . .'

Before Ronnie could fully digest Charlie's loyalty to him, the Bradshaws came back through the doorway. Bernie was smiling, which made Ronnie's heart beat fast enough; but what rolled him over and dried him up was the hard look of open hatred which Roy gave him as he followed behind. It was like looking into a cold steel muzzle. The man wouldn't easily forgive being dropped in it by the boy, his look said.

145

'Right,' Bernie said to Ronnie, 'now for old times' sake, being 'ow we're both fond of Stevie ... and Val ... we're gonna give you the benefit. Right? Perhaps you 'ave been a bit more sensible than what it looks. But you've gotta keep a hundred miles away from that girl, right? And later on Roy here, quite natural, ain't taking a chance on you skating round 'ere when 'e's over the other side with Charlie and the coach....' Bernie looked round, but Roy didn't bother to nod: his look was unaltered, like a hard kid not being got round by a teacher. 'So Charlie gets you one o' them identity card things an' you go with them.' He turned to the coach driver, all smarmy now. 'As a matter of fact, Charlie, it'll 'elp to look more natural, you sneakin' a seat for your grandson, or something. It'll all 'elp comin' back through the port.'

Charlie nodded. 'Yeah, O.K.,' he said. 'But I ain't 'appy about none of it, mind....'

'Yeah.' Bernie turned to go. Then he suddenly swung back at Ronnie, and with the undisguised anger of someone who has been forced to compromise, he growled, 'And don't push your luck no further, son! Or I might forget 'ow fond I am of Stevie, and sort you out once and for all....'

And they were gone.

The three of them left in the room stood motionless. Then, 'Bruce!' Charlie said when they'd heard the gate squeak shut.

Ronnie followed him out to find the animal lying asleep on the concrete, untidy like dead, with its limbs splayed out where the sudden chop had taken them.

'Leave 'im, 'e'll come to. I thought they might 'ave topped 'im.' Charlie folded his arms, looked at his coaches, and sighed forcefully. 'A right bloody turn out!' he said.

Ronnie sniffed, and turned away.

'Oh, it's all right, son. It weren't your fault—no more'n it's mine.' The man put a strong driver's hand on Ronnie's shoulder. 'It's just ...' his watery eyes looked up into the grey evening sky above dockland . . . 'it's just, like, typical, mate. . . .'

He led the way indoors with his heavy arm round Ronnie, warm, and close, and smelling of engines; with a strength and yet a gentleness which turned Ronnie over. This bloke couldn't hurt a fly: that wasn't his way. He hadn't flown at him, even grumbled at him, for dropping them all in it; instead, he felt sorry, and put his arm round him, like a fellow mourner. He was all right, Charlie.

Later, after a huge meal, Ronnie went out to clean the coach, just to be on his own for a bit. When he went through the door he found that Bruce wasn't up to barking at him very much, and he cautiously patted the dog's back, well away from the tender head.

He was going to walk on; but he didn't; he stayed. There was something warm and comforting about the patting, the physical contact with a living creature, and Ronnie patted some more.

'All right, Brucie, good boy,' he said, keeping a careful eye on the long teeth in the black gums. 'It's only me. Good boy.' He went on for some time like that, and gradually he found himself thinking his thoughts at the dog, telling to him, in his mind, what he couldn't tell to Charlie.

It would all have been all right, now, wouldn't it, Bruce, except for one thing? Except for Kingsland: him knowing, and me telling him.

He sniffed, and crouched down on a level with the dog.

But it weren't my fault. How was I to know Charlie wasn't bent and in with the Bradshaws? Only natural to think that, wasn't it? At the time?

He ran his hand along the dog's side, and then down one leg to finger the claws.

But I can't tell him, can I? Because if I do he won't go; *we* won't go; and then no one'll get done for it, and my dad won't ever come out.

Ronnie crouched there, suddenly wondering at being that

close to the fierce animal without feeling afraid. Then his mind went back to Charlie, and to Steve.

It really came down to one or the other, didn't it? It came down to stopping Charlie going inside, or getting Steve out. Because that would be the rotten upshot. If they went to France, Charlie would be bound to get done by the law coming back.

It should've been easy to decide; and in a way it was. There was never any doubt that Steve would win for Ronnie. What was it they said, blood was thicker than water? And Steve had got to be shown it wasn't Ronnie who'd shopped him with the reading card. Somehow, whatever else went off, Ronnie had to make up for that last hateful parting in the flat. But for all that, all the over-riding reasons for coming down on Steve's side, nothing would stop the painful feeling of treachery he got when he thought about Charlie walking—or driving—into a trap which he had helped to set....

Ronnie stood up and gently, very cautiously, ran a light finger down the dog's snout, flying it away when the dog moved slightly; then back again.

Besides, Ronnie told the big eyes, the Bradshaws were going to get done if it all went through, and that was important. Bloody important.

An angry feeling, allied to fear, welled up in his stomach, a sudden internal explosion of frustration and hate at everything that had happened to him because the Bradshaws existed.

Getting them was worth everything, every sacrifice. Even Charlie, if it came to it. . . .

12

The St. Peter's Darby and Joan Club were going to enjoy themselves in Paris. It might be only a long week-end, but it was a week-end to be anticipated, savoured, and then remembered. From the first Ronnie could spot the difference between this group, waiting for the coach outside the church, and the usual elderly day trips which Charlie did at week-ends. The women were in their same pale coats and blue-grey hair, the men still in sports jackets and trousers, with shouldered raincoats: but these trippers weren't standing silently, eyeing each other sideways: these were together. They cheered when Charlie turned the coach round their corner: and they each had a small case of luggage.

Ronnie swallowed when he saw the cases. All those bright labels, they just reminded him what this trip was really all about: everyone going for a good time to cover up the grim and dangerous business of smuggling those Indians in the boot: it was like the sugar on the horrible pill which was going to do for Charlie.

But Ronnie didn't need any reminding of what this week-end was all about. Hadn't they spent three hours the night before adjusting the secret partition at the back of the boot, assembling the Dexion bunks, then taking the whole thing down to lie innocently in the lockers like the odd bits of this and that which any coach accumulates? Hadn't Roy made him help, telling him the plans, forcing him into it as a full-blooded accomplice? No, he wasn't likely to forget about why they were going. Nor was he ever likely to lose this gnawing of betrayal he felt whenever the big man said something nice to him.

149

'Thank Gawd,' said Charlie, with a professional look at the pavement, 'they ain't brought too much stuff. I was afraid they was going to bring the kitchen sink....' He pulled in to the kerb and with a hiss of air the doors opened.

The first in was the vicar, tall, grey, and crew-cut, with a blue sailor's jumper beneath his dog collar. To Ronnie he looked all ready for a day's cockling at Southend.

'Good morning, driver,' he said to Charlie, smiling and rubbing his hands together. 'All well?' He surveyed the coach, nodding approval at the luxury of air vents and white plastic head-rests. 'Very nice, very nice. And this is your grandson? Lucky for you we had a seat, eh?' He shook Ronnie's hand as if he were shaking a rope. 'Got your visitors' passports? I've checked all our senior citizens, and no one's forgotten anything, I'm pleased to say.'

'Yes, thanks, Vicar,' Charlie said, swinging out of his seat to start loading the cases. But Ronnie couldn't resist putting his hand to his back pocket to touch the important document. Well, it was proof that he was someone, wasn't it—that he had to be accounted for.

Behind the vicar Roy Bradshaw climbed the steps. ''Morning,' he said, with a curt nod. He didn't look at Ronnie.

'Oh, hello, Mr. Browning.' The vicar looked at Roy's Air France shoulder bag. 'My goodness, you're travelling light....'

But Roy didn't reply. He had already turned to draw forward a small, well-built man of about forty, scowling beneath his thick waved hair, a look which could have been either short sight or distrust. 'This is Mr. da Silva, our partner in the travel business. Like I said, we're out to develop this market, make ourselves known over there, an' all that....'

'Of course....'

'So we'll sit up the front. Only we're doing this trip a bit cheap on account of our coming over ourselves to sort things out for the future....'

'Of course, naturally. My people quite understand. They won't mind where you sit. And they're all very grateful to you, Mr. Browning, you can be sure of that....'

'Yeah. Fine. And Mr. da Silva hopes you don't mind if he leaves his car up that crack alongside the church.'

'No, that's fine. I can quite easily park in the front on Sunday....'

Ronnie was frowning. Mr. Browning and Mr. da Silva! Who the small bloke was, God knew, but Roy Bradshaw-Browning looked about as much like a proper businessman as his Aunt Fanny, dressed like that in a thin floral shirt and old jeans. God, these vicars were dead easy to fool. But then everyone was, he supposed.

The two non-smiling men sat themselves in the double seat next to the driver's and immediately began talking in low voices. Ronnie couldn't hear them from his own seat behind Charlie; but from the way Mr. da Silva was going on, reporting something to Roy, Ronnie guessed he was the bloke who'd fixed it all up in France. He was probably telling Roy about the Indians being there for the pick-up, Ronnie reckoned. Something like that.

The old people got on, a bit impatient by now, but they soon bucked up again, and after each laboured pull up the steps they sorted themselves into their seats around Ronnie with cheerful repartee.

''Ello, son, you off to gay Paree an' all?'

'Lovely chara, i'n it? Comfy.'

'Mind your titfer, Wally.'

'You 'aving the window, May?'

Then the vicar checked them all again, and wished them a good time. There was a lot of laughing.

'We'll send you a card, Mr. Scott. Not too rude.'

'Thank you. Safe journey. We'll pray for you. See you back on Sunday night.'

'You hope, Vicar. He hopes, don't he?'

And then with few further words a quiet Charlie showed

151

them how the vents worked, closed the door on the vicar, and the coach went off to frail waves and back-to-schooldays cheers.

Going through the Dartford Tunnel and down the M2, listening to them, Ronnie could see how these people were an ideal cover-up for what was going on. They were stupid, he thought, trying to sing old songs and forgetting the words, keeping on at him with chocolate and sweets, all making the same stupid joke about Paris having to watch out when they got there. No one would think in a million years there was anything crooked going on under their fat old backsides. He ignored them as much as he could and scowled out of the window beside him.

Where was Kingsland now? he wondered. Was he following in a fast car? Was the helicopter that hovered over the motorway just counting the traffic like Charlie said, or was someone up there keeping an eye on this particular coach? Who knew? One thing seemed fairly certain, though. Roy Bradshaw and Mr. da Silva weren't worried. They weren't looking out for anything suspicious. They hardly glanced up from their smoke-shrouded conversation all the way to Dover.

Going across into France Ronnie found it hard to believe that anybody official knew the first thing about what was going on. His heart started to beat faster as they got off the coach and walked through the passport control on to the ship: but that was just the tension of being tallied with his photograph by the unsmiling man, nothing else. There was no hint of anything the least bit special going on. He'd been left in the dark by Kingsland since that day, only guessing that his movements were being checked, and now, as in those past weeks, whoever was doing it was being really clever about it. There was no sign of anyone watching them from behind a newspaper or anything, no Kingsland; and Roy Bradshaw went through on his passport made out to 'Browning' without a second glance. So the mood of the old people took everything over, and with all of them laughing at their criminal-looking photographs, everyone was a crook, and then no one, and it was hard to believe what the Bradshaw mob were really about that week-end.

Eventually, the ship gently released her hold on the quayside and Charlie emerged from securing the vehicle down below. And then Ronnie felt bad again, really bad, about what he was having to do to this decent old bloke.

'Well, what d'you think of it?' he asked Ronnie—as if he, too, had forgotten.

'Not all that different to the ferry over Woolwich,' Ronnie shrugged. ''Cept bigger. An' you 'ave to 'ave these passports....'

'Yeah,' said Charlie, squinting out to sea. 'You 'ave to 'ave those. You can say that again!'

On the run south from Boulogne almost everyone in the coach told everyone else that Charlie was driving on the wrong side of the road. It passed down the coach like a parcel, and Ronnie could almost feel the ache in Charlie's cheeks where he had to keep on smiling. He wanted to shut them all up like Miss Neame did at school. But which side of the road they drove on wasn't the difference between England and France which stayed with Ronnie the most. The difference Ronnie remembered—and would remember for a long time—was the one he'd spotted almost as soon as they'd berthed, strapped to the hip of the first French policeman in Customs: the huge, obvious, pistol on the chewing gendarme with the cold stare. Oh, God! Ronnie had taken a deep breath and walked quickly past him, not a step out of line: and two hours later he still sniffed and swallowed nervously at the thought of being caught on the wrong side by someone tooled-up like that.

They were doing a steady, rhythmic fifty down the A6 autoroute and the pensioners were beginning to doze, when Roy suddenly scraped to his feet and took the battered

153

microphone from Charlie's dashboard. He blew into it a couple of times, counted out loud, and, when he was sure he was being heard, he made his first bald contact of the day with the passengers.

'Right, regarding the arrangements,' he said, as if he made curt amplified announcements every day of his life, 'you can eat your packed dinners when you like an' we'll stop for you-know-what in about half-hour's time. Then it's straight on to the hotel outside Paris where we 'ave our tea and supper and settle in. You make your own amusements tonight....'

Someone cheered, and the embarrassing thought of them all clustered round an upright piano flickered into Ronnie's head for a second, before Roy's stone eyes told them all there'd be none of that.

'In the morning, early, we get straight down into Paris in the coach, and Mr. da Silva here does a tour round with us, showing us places, and we're all booked in a night-club till we've 'ad enough. Then it's back to the hotel, a good kip, an' the coach leaves for 'ome at....'

He looked at Mr. da Silva, who muttered, 'Nine a.m. in the morning. French time.'

'Nine a.m. in the morning.' He frowned, and looked at the stopped clock of the coach. 'Oh, yeah, by the way, French time is an hour different, so you've gotta change your watches. The time now, in France,' he looked at his own watch on its wide, leather, strap, 'is two p.m. An hour on. Right, then we arrive back at Shepherds Gate at approximately twelve midnight, English time. All right? Right.'

Carelessly he left the microphone dangling, and after answering a couple of queries about the watches going on or back, he sat down next to Mr. da Silva and set about altering his own watch. Ronnie, his own eyes glazed with sleep, watched him. Everything about this hard threat of a man drew his attention, as a rotten apple draws ants, and even the thought of Charlie being caught up in bother and the trouble coming to the black girl's father, couldn't really take away from the terrific feeling Ronnie got when he thought of Roy being arrested as they got back to Dover on Sunday. That was going to be worth a bit of suffering for.

The small gold watch on the over-wide strap was a fiddle for Roy's big fingers, and Ronnie watched, dreamy and hypnotized, as the man nursed his left arm in his lap to take the whole thing off.

Great banana fingers! Fancy putting a stupid little watch like he'd got on a dirty great strap like that!

And then it happened. Roy had the watch carefully cradled in his right hand when a small French car with more ambition than power suddenly cut in on the coach as it overtook.

'Watch it, idiot!'

'Bloody madman!'

Charlie, swearing, had to stamp briefly on the brakes, hard enough to make everyone throw a hand forward to steady themselves on something in front.

'Worse than your boy, Wally!'

Ronnie's hand shot to the back of Charlie's seat. Stupid berk!

Roy Bradshaw grabbed at the dashboard with his free left hand. 'Stupid little frog!'

And for Ronnie that changed everything. For while Charlie shouted 'Sorry!' to the coach, and Roy went on some more about 'Bloody frog drivers!', Ronnie looked across to see Roy's anger, drawn by the fascination of a safe sort of fear. But he didn't see the contorted face or the long grey teeth, instead his eyes were drawn to the strong, bare mahogany left wrist which was thrusting forward, to the wide strip of contrasting white skin where the strap had been—where, like a birth-mark, a fading but unmistakeable stripe of indelible purple paint stood out. It took a few seconds to impress itself: and then with a sudden feeling of being frozen Ronnie realized. The spray! What Kingsland had been on about when they'd arrested Steve. The stuff sprayed on in the City East raid.

Bloody hell! So that was the reason for the wide strap: not the stupid look of it, or a bad arm, but a cover-up for the tell-tale sign that Roy Bradshaw had been in on the football job!

Jesus Christ!

As Roy looked round quickly to see who'd seen, Ronnie looked away out of the window, fighting to breathe, only just keeping himself from clouting Charlie on the shoulder and telling him there and then to stop the coach. His heart pounded and his throat felt big. God! This was something and a half, wasn't it? But keep calm, sit bloody still, don't give the game away. What did it mean? You had to think it all out. You had to be clever, you had to think it all through before you did anything. He'd done himself by going off too quickly once before.

He took deep breaths, and he frowned, thinking hard as a regular line of French trees went past in a blur. Take it easy. It was no good chasing down the wrong road now.

Right, he thought, now this made a big difference, didn't it? Definitely, because unless he was dead wrong that purple spray definitely meant Roy Bradshaw could be got for the City East job. It had to! So now he could be got for two things! For that as well as for this black smuggling. And it only needed Ronnie to tell him where to look and Kingsland could throw the book at him!

Hold on! A new excitement suddenly straightened his back as it hit him. Yeah, when *he* told Kingsland! Him, Ronnie! When Kingsland knew who it was who'd fingered Bradshaw—Ronnie Webster, not Charlie, or a French copper with a gun, or anyone else—then *he'd* be the one who came in for the reward. Not money, but the deal: the special treatment he'd been promised for Steve.

Yeah! Too right! Ronnie was excited. Between glances at grim Roy—*fingered* Roy—he fidgeted on his seat, turned this way and that and looked at his keen eye in the mirroring window, and for five minutes he badly wanted to tell someone: to whisper in Charlie's ear; or, if he could have written, to have slipped a note to him. But he couldn't write, and there was no whispering in this noisy coach, especially not to the driver, so he just had to wait. And as the coach resumed its rhythmic fifty his thoughts went spiralling on and another, deeper significance gradually occurred to him.

It did change everything, that wrist, but it changed things even more than he'd just worked out; because surely to God he'd got enough now to help Steve *without having to get Bradshaw for the smuggling.* The City East job would be enough, wouldn't it? It wouldn't be ideal for Kingsland, but it would be enough for Steve. And that way he could let Charlie off the hook altogether. Yeah! Because Charlie couldn't get done by the police for what he didn't do, could he? Ronnie started to chew a finger-nail. Right! So that meant they didn't need to pick up the Indians at all!

Great! A surge of light-headedness, like a sudden acceleration in Steve's car, brought a tight smile of contentment to Ronnie's thin face. Roy Bradshaw would still be getting done for a bloody big robbery; and a hundred to one it'd rope in Bernie Bradshaw too. Enough to put them both down for a hell of a long time and all! He crossed his legs as this strange new feeling of relief made him want to urinate. He looked across at Roy again, but with a sudden new sense of power over him now: at the tight face staring dead ahead out of the window; at the strong arms crossed and the watch well hidden. Bloody got you! he thought. Because I know! It was like seeing Miss Neame's secret scratches, this having something on somebody. It was like beating the clever Bradshaws at their own game. Now all he had to do was get Charlie on his own and tell him, and get him to somehow put a stop to it. Great! It was all over now bar the shouting: and there'd be plenty of that to come!

But at the services area it somehow all went off the boil. Charlie was so busy at the diesel pump, with Mr. da Silva alongside him going on at the garage bloke in French, that Ronnie couldn't get near him. Instead, he had to try to look purposeful and innocent for Roy Bradshaw, and with the old ladies all round, whooping about the different sort of lavatory and offering him strange foreign sweets they'd bought, he realized with a sinking feeling that they'd all be at the place where they were sleeping before he stood any chance of getting his urgent news to Charlie.

But Ronnie couldn't think of anything else, and after a short sleep in the warm drone of the coach and a sudden awakening in different surroundings, in a different frame of mind, Ronnie began to go over it all yet again: but now he began to realize that perhaps not getting to Charlie at the services stop had been the best thing that could have happened. And the more he thought about it the more he realized that he'd had a very narrow escape from making another big mistake. The scenery helped. In his hopeful mood after the discovery, they'd been going through rolling green countryside, with the sun shining and the coach bowling along. But now they were in traffic, crawling through the industrial build-up of north Paris, looking out at the sunless streets which were much more like home. It was all much more realistic, and in a new, flatter mood, Ronnie could begin to see that it had been a huge stroke of luck that he hadn't told Charlie anything.

He was sitting up dead straight, with his nose flat to the cold window. What the hell could have got hold of him before? When he looked ahead a bit, beyond the end of his stupid nose, he could see that even if he told him there was nothing Charlie could do about anything. Well, was there? he asked himself. If he put himself in Charlie's shoes and forgot about his own side of things for a minute he could see there was no way Charlie could wriggle out of doing what he was being forced to do. If Ronnie told him, and did what he'd have to—told him about the police knowing about the whole thing—how could Charlie call it off? He couldn't just go and tell Roy Bradshaw and Mr. da Silva that the police would be waiting for them when they got back, could he? No way! That'd be the end of Ronnie Webster, no bloody doubt. And Charlie couldn't just tell them he wouldn't do it, that he'd changed his mind—or that'd be the end of him, wouldn't it? Ronnie scowled at a grim pavement café. So what the hell could he do? He sniffed, and rubbed his eyes violently. Christ! It wasn't stinking fair, was it? Nothing was. Not the whole rotten business for a start, and then specially not having had this gift of a piece of vital information stuck under his nose till he was so deep in a mess that the right thing was just about impossible to do! Like one of them mirage efforts, he thought, the end to his troubles kept coming up in front of him, and then kept vanishing out of the way at the last minute.

He looked out of the front window and started to chew at his nails again. From a seat behind him, another life altogether, someone laughed, some old dear seeing something different, and funny, out in the French street.

'Here, Glad, that'd do for your Mavis!'

There were mild whoops of laughter, Ronnie didn't know what about—but at least it served to make him suddenly remember the presence of all the old people. Here! What about telling one of them? Could one of the old dears fix it for him? He sneered at the window. Nah! He rejected the idea straight away. Daft! They wouldn't believe him for a start; and they were all too stupid, anyway; all their silly ways, and stupid sayings. He was more sensible than they were, any day of the week, even if he couldn't bloody read!

All right Mr. Clever! So if he was more sensible than them, what about him, then? The idea hit him as suddenly as indigestion. So why couldn't *he* put the kibosh on the whole thing, ruin it in some way, cock it up so it couldn't go ahead? Couldn't he sling away the Dexion, or something?

159

He thought about it hard, his stomach turning again with a new sort of fear as his brain fought with the risky, impossible ideas. No, they'd only buy some more Dexion, find some more hardboard, lash something up.

But something was on, wasn't it? If he was worth anything he'd work something out to help Steve and Charlie—something to put this animal in front where he belonged.

Well, he bloody was worth something! And he'd do it! Somehow. He shifted in his seat, and shivered. But Christ knew how. He didn't.

Ronnie didn't puzzle away at his problem for long. He never did. Either a solution came quite quickly or he let it go, hoping that something would come along to solve it. It was a way of life, and that was what so many teachers never understood. But there wasn't time anyway because now, very quickly, they pulled up at a small dark hotel, an old building crumbling in a narrow crumbling street, an area of tight turns where Charlie needed all his skill to manoeuvre the coach into a close-fitting alley. The pensioners, tired and becoming irritable after the long journey, clamoured to be first off and then milled round the back of the coach, uncertain, bagging Ronnie in turn to help them with their cases. And one after another, tired as he was, he made the journey up strange dim stairs, banging doors open with the cases, his lack of care scuffing the wood with marks of red, blue, and tan plastic, until, after a chaotic half-hour, the old people were settled in their rooms with pots of foreign lemon tea, and Ronnie found himself shunted off into a small room no bigger than a cupboard with a squat bottle of Orangina.

God alive! It suddenly struck him as he sucked alone—what the hell was he doing here? This was crazy, a nightmare! Over France, all alone in this room, with Roy Bradshaw down the corridor and his only friend, old Charlie, too busy doing what he was told to even come and talk to him!

160

Restless with fatigue, Ronnie prowled and swigged; looked under the bed and in the small cupboard; went to the window to push open the shutters; and to his surprise he suddenly found himself looking down at the coach, which stood like a large resting animal in the alley below. Already, long before sunset, the alley was dark and gloomy, and Ronnie grudgingly had to hand it to Mr. da Silva for choosing this place; it was ideal for what they had to do—fixing up the coach on the quiet. Once someone was at one of the side lockers or round the back, there wouldn't even be room for anyone else to stand and watch, and in all that dank gloom no one would be spotted at work anyway.

Ronnie looked up and down the alley, at the ancient crumbling wall on either side of the window, at the pitted plaster and the rough stone beneath. The place looked as if it hadn't been repaired for years. These had to be shell holes from the war, he thought. The way they ran in a line sideways down the wall. He'd seen films on the telly made in places like this. This'd be just the place where someone'd jump down and shove a long knife up to the handle in some Gestapo's guts. Great! He enjoyed the thought and suddenly his hands couldn't keep still, and he picked at the wall with the same nervous movement that had worried the plastic off a reading card, the stuffing out of a chair at home.

Crash!

What the hell! He jumped, as his restless fingers suddenly sent a large piece of stone crashing down into the alley, a heavy missile that narrowly missed the coach and fell with the thud of an unexploded bomb on to the cobbles.

God! Good job Charlie hadn't been down there, or one of the old dears: it would have killed them, easy. He looked back at the wall. Another huge piece of rough stone hung there exposed, and it'd take next to nothing to send that crashing down after the first. Bloody dangerous! He breathed less heavily. He'd have to watch out in future.

Ronnie pulled the shutters closed and sat in the dark

slatted room, finishing the Orangina with loud snorts of the straw. Then as the wear of the travelling and the fatigue of the excitement caught up with him again, he laid down on the narrow bed, and within minutes he'd drifted off into a restless, troubled sleep; and everything else, even knocking on Charlie's door for a grim smile, had to wait.

Some while later the nag of a headache woke him in the small, airless room. It was dark, his mouth was dry, and he had no idea of the time. He was unsettled. Perhaps he'd been dreaming about it all, he didn't know; but he lay there, thinking about the black girl's father and the others lying in those cramped bunks, one on top of another in the dark, hot boot; and he thought about them now, that minute, probably lying on beds like this in some dingy place up near the sea, waiting for the time to go, thinking about making it to the coach at the right time, in the right place. Hiding, waiting in the dark, it was all horrible. And the stupid thing was, if he could manage to do what he wanted, it'd all be a waste of their time anyway: because it was all down to him to stop them getting anywhere near Dover.

They had to be desperate to be doing it; but not nearly as desperate as he was to stop it.

The hot, stale place wrapped tight round his head. He shuddered, suddenly wanting to shout, and with a jerky lunge at the clinging black blanket of claustrophobia, he fought his way off the bed and found the shutters, urgently throwing them open.

There was an impatient thump at the door. It opened fast before Ronnie had time to turn from the window. Roy Bradshaw stood silhouetted against the dull light of the corridor.

'Come on!' he growled. 'Want your meal, doncha? I've 'ad mine. You can 'ave yours quick an' 'elp me start checking the stuff in the coach—while all the old 'uns are inside 'avin' theirs. You know I've gotta make sure we're all set for Sunday, an' there won't be no time tomorrow. We've gotta be away sharp to time Sunday or we'll miss the pick-up. They won't 'ang about long.' He looked round Ronnie's room with his nose, as if he knew Ronnie was planning something. 'Come on, 'urry up, I shan't ask twice. I told you, Sonny Jim, you're in this as much as anyone. . . .'

Abruptly, Roy went, and Ronnie kicked the door shut behind him. Pick the bones out of that! God, if only he could think of a way to screw this up for him: make him really go through it, and then get him arrested in the end. If only he could think of a good way. The sweet aroma of revenge filled his head like the fumes of a forbidden cigarette, and he inhaled. God, if only. . . .

A faint sound in the alley beneath took him quickly back to the window, and he looked down to see Bradshaw sidling along by the side of the coach, stopping and stooping just to Ronnie's right to open the side locker. Ronnie rolled a big gob in his mouth. Wouldn't he like to—right on his head! He could, if he leaned further over. What wouldn't he like to do to Roy Bradshaw, one of the causes of everything; one of the two, Ronnie thought, who'd got him and God-knew-how-many East End families living in fear and trembling.

He swallowed; while below, Roy's hard, rough face twisted and his close eyes squinted as he sorted out the metal strips, oblivious to quite where he was, with no idea of Ronnie leaning out of the window above him.

Ronnie shifted, and a small piece of surface plaster was dislodged and fell, fluttering down, too light to be noticed. But it made Ronnie look nervously again at the wall, drawing his eyes for the second time to the large, sharp piece of masonry which badly wanted to fall.

And Ronnie suddenly saw it. The way out. The answer he'd been waiting for. The terrible accident which could pay Roy Bradshaw out—perhaps for good-and-all—and lead to the whole business being called off! Charlie would be left in the clear; and the paint-spray evidence would still be on Bradshaw's wrist like a tattoo, plenty good enough to make Kingsland see that Steve got a fair deal.

Ronnie tasted the iron of blood in his mouth. His heart beat faster. Could he? Was he up to doing it? It'd be easy, wouldn't it? He couldn't miss from here, could he? And it'd bloody finish Bradshaw for certain. His chest felt tight again, and he became excited, light-headed, the tips of his teeth tingling. A paying-back, a proper drop of rough justice: and no one to blame him for it! All he had to do after was just shut his window and go downstairs, all innocent, for his supper. He breathed faster, began to pant, as he saw the stone falling, digging its weight into Bradshaw's bullet head. Well, it was no more than what the Bradshaws would do in his place, was it? And what was good enough for them was good enough for him!

Ronnie reached round for the stone. Yeah. He screwed his face up, tough. Then he'd be just like them, wouldn't he? Ruthless, and someone to be reckoned with. Someone little kids'd be scared of—because he'd let on in the end, who'd done it, when the Bradshaw lot were all out of the way. Definitely. Yeah! It was the only way to do things when you were dealing with animals like these. Get them before they got you.

He felt the primitive cutting edge of heavy flint beneath his fingers, and he glanced down at the oblivious, crouching man.

It was just what they'd all do themselves, wasn't it? Roy, Bernie Bradshaw, Mr. da Silva, probably Charlie.

No, not Charlie. He caught his breath, stopped for a moment as if some current had been suddenly reduced. No, he thought, not Charlie; definitely not. Tough and frightening he might have seemed once, but he was different underneath. Ronnie could vouch for that, as the memory flashed into his head of the man in his yard, of the strong hand on his shoulder, the close smell of the engine: of Charlie who repaired, instead of breaking up. No, dropping the stone wouldn't be Charlie's way. Charlie could have been really rough on him after the Bradshaws' visit if he'd wanted to be; but instead he'd winked, and smiled, and been gentle....

And Steve, too. Steve wasn't really Bradshaws' sort, was he? He'd be quick, fly, and crafty, but one of the safest drivers on the track. No, Steve didn't settle things in blood.

So what to bloody do? Who to be like? Suddenly he just didn't know any more.

Scowling, frustrated, vigorously rubbing a deep itch on his leg, Ronnie turned back into the room, leaving the flint to hang where it was for a bit longer, clenching and unclenching his hands with the nervous energy of indecision. He looked at the tumbled bed, and once more he breathed in the anxious, claustrophobic atmosphere of the room. He spun back and looked out again: was he too late? But in that instant the moment had passed: he knew it as it happened, and he stood, stock-still, and as he stood he thought once more of the Indian girl's father and the other men, waiting themselves, not to miss their own moment of action when it came.

And at that moment the new idea came suddenly to the surface, like a flashing fish in murky waters that had been lurking there for some time. Another possible way of doing it. Well, just possible.

He sat down on the bed and tried to make himself think, squeezing his eyes shut, frowning, and rocking.

Yeah. That was it. He sniffed sardonically, as if he didn't believe it himself. It was simple: dead simple, the idea. Thinking of those Indians and their timing had given it to him; just like that, on a plate. Another way that could get the same result without blood spreading all over the alley. Granted, doing it would be tricky, and dangerous: but then nothing was safe these days: and it would be Charlie Whitelaw's way, and not Roy Bradshaw's.

Decided now, he got up off the bed; and within three minutes he was downstairs tucking noisily into a beef casserole; and within twelve he was outside in the alley helping Roy Bradshaw with the Dexion, keeping a watchful eye on the dangerous wall above. He'd been faced-about yet again; but this time, he knew he'd made the move himself.

13

When they got back from Paris the next night Ronnie didn't hang about downstairs. He made straight for his room, and his bed. It was good to be out of the way: the best place, he decided, with Charlie suddenly all uptight about the smuggling job and Roy Bradshaw going about all day with Mr. da Silva, the pair of them looking as if they were ready to attack anyone who even glanced in their direction. Ronnie was tired, anyway, and he knew that to do what he wanted to do he needed to rest up early on in the night.

The trip round Paris had been a drag, all up and down steps which half the old dears couldn't tackle; so instead of having a bit of time for Ronnie, Charlie had been left with puffing old people to look after all day, and with parking places to find everywhere they went. And at the end of it all the night-club had been a real let-down: too tame, Ronnie thought, with all the dirty jokes in a language none of them could understand. But at least everyone was tired out at the end of it, and the snores and moans on the way back told Ronnie they'd all sleep well that night. And that was important.

Worry kept Ronnie from sleeping, though, even from dozing the hour he was prepared to allow himself. The nag of going over why he hadn't done what he should have done and smashed Bradshaw's head like an egg-shell, the nervousness of waiting to get going, the whole responsibility for mucking up their plans, kept his legs twitching and his eyes wide open in the dark. So for what seemed to be the thousandth time that day he went over the Bradshaws' plan for the pick-up.

It was all quite slick really, and if he'd been on their side he'd have felt well pleased with the way it was all worked out. But he wasn't, and so knowing the plan was his big bonus.

First, the boot had to be got ready; fixing up three Dexion bunks, one on top of the other, behind the false panel. Well, they'd done that the night before, and the boot was locked. So there was nothing he could have done to muck that up. But what was to happen next was where he stood his chance, and this he could have recited in his sleep, like a bit of Miss Neame's poetry.

In the morning, after they'd had their breakfast, the boot would get loaded up with the cases, and off they'd go back to the coast. But before they got to Boulogne Charlie was supposed to pull off the road up a side-way near a special café and say he'd got a flat tyre. Then Roy Bradshaw was going to make sure all the old people stayed on the coach while Charlie, Mr. da Silva, and Ronnie ran round and threw the cases out of the back—pretending to get the spare wheel—at the same time as the three Indians came out from where they were hiding and bundled into their bunks behind the partition. Then it was cases back and all aboard again to the docks.

It was all worked out, and definitely not hard to do. Like all the best schemes it was dead simple. But—and this was the thing, Ronnie kept telling himself—if anything went wrong, if someone was on to them, or it was too dangerous for some reason, the coach was going to shoot straight past and miss the café out. That was the arrangement. Then the three Indians were going to have to clear off out of the area and either take their chances some other way or go back where they came from. So that gave everyone just two hours, between three and five, when the coach had got to

167

show up. And if it didn't it would just have to go back without them. They'd have to get shot of the partition somewhere on the way and carry on normally, just like any ordinary trip. And that was what Ronnie was banking on. Not showing up. No smuggling, no running any risks at all; not Bradshaw, not Mr. da Silva, and not Charlie.

Especially not Charlie, Ronnie told himself. If the coach didn't show up in time Charlie would be as safe as houses.

Ronnie turned over on his bed yet again and yawned nervously. It was all so easy when you just thought about it. All he had to do to make his plan work was just stop the coach from making it to the café in time. Easy! He rubbed his eyes in the dark. Well, it should be. The only worry had been *how* to do it—how to hold things up long enough at this end and keep the coach away from that café till after five....

He turned on his back and looked at the ceiling. And what about his answer to it? He sniffed another dry, nervous sniff. Well, he didn't know enough about engines to have thought for even a second about his chances of mucking the coach up so much that Charlie and the others couldn't put it right in time. And he'd guessed that let-down tyres wouldn't hold them back for long, either. So he'd had to think up something else. And after a lot more tossing and turning the night before, the card he'd finally decided to play was the one he'd turned down out of hand on the Friday. The passengers. The stupid old people who seemed to like kids so much. Now he was depending on them coming up trumps when it came to it. Because they'd rather miss the boat than go home without one of the passengers, wouldn't they? Of course they would. No doubt about it. None of that lot had to go to work the next day, so they'd have a marvellous time playing Bradshaw up if he tried to get the coach to go with one short—especially without the kid they'd all been making all the fuss of for the past two days. Without 'little Ronnie'. They'd all want to feel bad about that.

He turned on his front and stared down into a dip in the bolster. It was dead simple. It was. He didn't need to be scared. He was used to this sort of thing. He'd done it when Val had left home, and that had only been one time out of hundreds. He was used to going off, keeping himself out of everyone's way till things blew over. Past master at it, he was, so he didn't really have to worry about it. It was just that usually he did it as soon as he needed to, on the quick: and this time he'd been planning it, and had to wait for the right moment.

And tonight was when it was going to happen—well, early in the morning when everyone was dead asleep. That was when he was going to go out of the door, past Bradshaw's room, and Charlie's, and Mr. da Silva's, down the front stairs to the alley: and then away: and lose himself in the back streets, just like in London. Till later, round about five o'clock, and then he'd see what he would do.

His face now hot in the bolster, he turned back over and imagined the scene by the coach outside: the first 'Where's the boy?'; the searching high and low in the hotel; the old dears getting off and not letting the coach go till all the proper things had been done; someone forcing one of the organizers to tell the police. Then the hold-ups, the statements: and all the while the two tough guys, Roy Bradshaw and Mr. da Silva, trying to get away and the old dears being stroppy, and refusing.

'No, mate, we ain't goin' till we've done what we can for the boy, poor little cock....'

''Ow can you *think* of going?'

'Wally'll lie down in front of them wheels if you try goin' without the boy—won't you, Wally?'

Ronnie had to have a sardonic smile. He could picture it all, hear all the comments, see all the old outraged faces. Yeah, it'd work, he was sure of it. Well, anyway, he sniffed, there was damn all to lose by trying. Once he was along at the end of this landing, past Bradshaw's door, he was away, wasn't he? They couldn't do any harm to him once he was past that door, because they'd never bloody catch him. And getting past there should be easy enough in the early hours of the morning, when everyone else was dead asleep....

There was a town clock somewhere nearby sounding out the quarters, and while Ronnie lay there waiting through the hours he could hear the chimes coming closer through the quietening houses and the thinning traffic. He listened for every one, every quarter, because he knew he had to. He was so drugged with tiredness after that long day round Paris that he had to fight to keep his head up, and listening for the chimes helped him to keep a check on his own consciousness. He wasn't running the risk of nodding off and being woken up next morning by Bradshaw, or Charlie, too late to do a bunk in the dark. It'd all be useless in daylight because Bradshaw and da Silva would soon catch him if it was only speed that counted. No, he had to get away at the right time: before they all got up in the hotel, and after early people had started going to work. That way he wouldn't look like some night-time crook and get picked up by one of those coppers with the guns. About a quarter to five would do it, he reckoned. Or half-past four.

It was a lifetime ringing round: and he thought he'd remember those bells for the rest of his days, coming in through those shutters like a personal message, ringing out just for him. He missed a quarter, sometime after two, and for a while he thought the clock had gone wrong. But it hadn't: he'd momentarily lost his battle against sleep, and been back in his flat, in the old chair.... So he forced himself to sit up, and then stand up, and then prowl silently inside the small room to prevent it happening again. The worst part, though, towards the endless end, was the other fight within himself: the unforeseen battle between his will and his bladder. He'd guessed he might have a battle to keep awake, but he hadn't thought about this. And he should have. God, he should have known. . . . By three o'clock, after all that Orangina at the night-club, he badly wanted to go along to the toilet; but he knew that he daren't risk disturbing Bradshaw before he made his break. So he searched desperately around the room, one hand clutching at himself, but there was nothing he could use, no vase or waste bin, and he had to hold it, crossing and uncrossing his legs, swearing softly as he rocked, and sweated. But at least his agony was keeping him awake all the time.

He held out till the clock had struck a quarter past four, and then he couldn't wait a minute longer. He had to move. He had to get going and get outside. It was desperate. And anyway, he thought, it was about time now; or as good as. . . .

He made sure his visitors' passport was still in his back pocket, and he fingered the francs Charlie had given him which he hadn't spent. Then he put on his leather bomber, which seemed to creak out of its creases loud enough to wake Paris, and he tiptoed to the door.

Now for it. He was off. God, he hoped Charlie would thank him for this, because it was a hell of a lot more touch-and-go now that it came to it! He put his hand on the uncertain door-knob, and all at once he felt drained of energy, low and dispirited. This was when they shot people, or chopped their heads off, wasn't it? Or raided their houses. Early, when they had no fight in them. He put his head to the crack. Some kids'd probably just go down to the lav and then come back to kip, he thought, if it was just down to them. He breathed in deeply. But he'd made his mind up. He was going to keep Charlie out of bother—or have a bloody good crack at it, anyhow. He owed him a try, didn't he?

Slowly, with his eyes screwed tight against the sound, he turned the handle and opened the door, just wide enough to squeeze through. He led with his head, and he opened his eyes.

The narrow landing was a dim blue, like the sleeping lights on posh coaches: and it was all very, very, quiet, with a silence like the hiss of a blank cassette in his ears.

To his left were some dark stairs which no one seemed to use—God knew where they went; directly opposite was Charlie's door; and two metres along was Roy Bradshaw's; while beyond that, like the open door out of a prison, were the proper stairs which led down through two floors to the ground: stairs which led to the front door and to the maze of streets which would hide him.

Ronnie had the eerie feeling that with everyone entombed in sleep he was the only living thing on earth. Please God, if only they'd stay that way for the next few minutes!

Charlie's door didn't bother him. He'd be all right, the big man dead asleep in his little bed without Elsie. But Roy Bradshaw's did, and as Ronnie crept along, tread by tread, he strained his eyes on it, watering them sore rather than blink in the dull blue light. He suddenly had an enormous urge to just run, like he had in the coach that night, screaming his head off down the stairs, letting it all out: but he fought it, and held himself shivering in check, and screwed up his toes and lightened his feet as he trusted himself to the thin carpet as if it were ice. A creak would be a crack, and he could be plunged into disaster if the man were lying awake on his bed. Ronnie—the slight figure smaller than ever alone out there on the landing—took another hesitant step, picturing the man in there in the dark, eyes open like a snake, lying there waiting to writhe out at the sound of movement. But with his seeing eyes Ronnie took in every mark on the blue-tinted door; the dark purple smoothness round the handle where everyone touched, the dark smudge of suitcase scuffs lower down, the strange French seven with the bar. All his senses heightened now, Ronnie missed nothing. Roy Bradshaw in there, the boy thought, a couple of steps away on the other side of that bit of wood! Get past here and he'd never ever see him again! Except in the paper, with his brother, when they were done for the football job.

Step; stare; step. And even as Ronnie stared, creeping his

way along the landing, silently, smoothly, and as sinister as the cemetery gates, Bradshaw's door swung slowly open and there the man stood, fully dressed, his hair all over his face and his eyes shining unnaturally bright, as if his body was kept awake by some other force controlling him; a science-fiction creature within another's power.

Ronnie just stopped, block-frozen, stomach tearing, his head pounding; everything inside reacting, but his limbs numb, his feet iced to the floor. Total shock. He'd known it would happen, hadn't he? Had the things he was most scared of always got to be so real that they *had* to happen? one detached part of his brain wanted to know.

Drugs. Ronnie had seen it as he froze. The man had been on something to keep him alert for so long. Hyped up, he was. And ten times as deadly.

'Where you goin'?' The voice was sharp, and thin. 'What's your little game?'

'Eh?'

'Where you goin', you little swine?'

'Toilet. I'm goin' toilet....' And in his numbness, Ronnie was aware that he *was* going, right there; his legs suddenly hot, and the uncontrolled urine trickling into a nervous pool at his feet.

'In your leather?'

'I was cold....' And now he *was* cold; but it was a real, physical feeling of coldness, a spasm triggered by his body reacting for him. He shivered. Already his legs were clammy wet and he stood there scared out of his mind, trapped, and degraded.

'Come in 'ere!'

What? But the state of shock had suddenly passed with the urine. Ronnie was becoming alert, feeling threatened, and ready to act. Go in there with him? He must be bloody joking!

'I said, come in 'ere!' Bradshaw hissed. 'I can read you like a bloody book. You ain't movin' out of my sight from

now on! I've 'ad all I'm taking from you! I've 'ad enough!'
His eyes were open wide now, and his face was white with
real anger. Roy Bradshaw had taken over his own body too,
from the automatic alertness of the drugs. 'Come in 'ere!'
He made an impatient, imperative gesture with his hand as
he hissed the words in the unconscious corridor.

Ronnie stared at him. God, what to do? This was it,
wasn't it? This was finally it! He'd got to do something quick,
for Crissake! He stared, and as his alert fugitive's mind raced,
he saw the black gap of the staircase at the edge of his
vision. But he knew without another second's thought that
that was out. He'd never make it past Bradshaw to those
stairs in a million years. The man could grab him easy. He'd
have him smeared all down the wall if he even tried to make
a move for it.

'Are you gonna do as I say or do I come an' get you?' Roy
Bradshaw's thin creased body had shifted to lean forward.
He meant business. Since that day in Charlie's kitchen he'd
had this grudge, and now was the time for settling it up. He
was coming at him, Ronnie knew. He could see it in his
squinting eyes. He could see he was only hesitating while he
thought out how he'd grab him to make the least noise....

Right, so he'd never make the stairs. Oiled on panic now,
Ronnie's brain raced. But what about diving back into his
own room, opening the shutters, and jumping on the roof of
the coach?

No, he'd never make it. While he opened the shutters and
climbed up the man'd be grabbing him round where it hurt.
Oh, God!

'Did you 'ear me?' Bradshaw hissed, with a last look over
his shoulder.

It was now, God, it was now!

Quick! Hold on! There were those other stairs behind him,
weren't there? At the other end of the corridor. Narrow
stairs, back stairs that no one ever used. He didn't
know where they went, except that they went down. But at

least that was half a chance....

'Right, you little swine!'

Roy Bradshaw spoke out now. He wasn't bothering to
keep his voice down. All the hatred was out in the open for
anyone to hear. This was it! Here he came!

'Get stuffed, Bradshaw!'

As Roy made his move, so did Ronnie. He was ready. He
spat; a dirty diversion which made Roy recoil and wipe
his face against his will. And then he turned and ran for the
narrow stairs like a fox with the hounds at his tail. In six
strides he was there, jumping at the post, stumbling round
the sharp bend to the next half-landing as Roy Bradshaw
reached, long-armed like disease, towards him. Ronnie took
flight in the way Steve had in the stolen car, eyes focused on
the next move, the next hand-hold, foot space: all his practised skills as a fugitive came into play, the swerving body,
the bent head, the battering shoulders. And with his run,
his final out-in-the-open defiance, suddenly came that same
sense of careless abandon he'd had as Steve's passenger, the
light-headed feeling that succeed or fail, live or even die,
what he was doing now was what he most had to do in all
the world: a full-up feeling of satisfaction.

Ronnie leapt regardless and Roy pursued; but Bradshaw's
feet were bigger and he was forced to slow and watch his
step as he rattled down. A dark door on the floor below
ended the staircase. Ronnie bashed through it and ran full
tilt back across the building, through a wide dust-sheeted
dining-room, disused out of season. Eyes wide, he ran in
scared softness across the sheeted floor, while behind him,
up on the other side of the stairs door, he could hear
Bradshaw coming, bumping, thumping, and cursing. Where
to? How the hell did he get out of this bare room? God, his
stomach churned, he'd run into a dead end! But no, thank
Christ! Ahead, as he covered the length of the room, by the
dim yellow lights above them, he saw two more doors; two
ways out of it, and each of them with a white painted sign.

The way down? Which one, for God's sake? One of them *had* to lead to the stairs, didn't it? Somehow? But the other? It could go into anywhere: a cupboard, a kitchen, an office. *And which was which?*

Oh, hell! He stopped before them, panicking a look round. There were no other doors on the floor, and there was nowhere in the white room where he could hide.

He had to make the right choice. Take the wrong door and he could end up in some dead-end room where Bradshaw could get him. And there wouldn't be any time for a second chance.

Quick! With a wild panic gorging in his stomach he heard the banging on the stairs behind him. Bradshaw was on the last twist, speeding up, caring less as he clattered down. Ronnie stared hard at the doors. His head spun from one to the other. Which one? The two signs, meaningless hieroglyphics in white paint, stared coldly at him. Words! They'd give the answer to some. But he couldn't bother with words: he couldn't read words: so he stared instead at the wood, because doors he *could* read: he'd spent his whole life finding ways round reading, hadn't he? Every door in the school had had to be read, and then remembered, without any help from the words painted on them.

Right door. A wide area of dark marks above the handle: push marks, like on the swing doors at school. Could be anywhere. The stairs. A kitchen. An office. All doors got pushed.

Left door. Push marks the same, but not so dark. And scuff marks from cases, low down. So people with luggage sometimes went through this door. Well, you didn't take cases into kitchens or offices. But if you worked for the hotel you might take a short cut through here with someone's stuff.

So, left. It was the only chance. Shivering scared now at the thought of Bradshaw pushing the door behind him any instant, Ronnie leapt at the one before him and ran on through, racing forward and throwing himself on down the stairs he knew would be there—and to his great relief he found himself back on the familiar staircase down to the lobby. Right! Right! He wanted to shout. He'd been bloody right!

A distant door slammed behind him as Roy Bradshaw got into the disused dining-room, and Ronnie went on break-neck down, risking everything, twisted ankle, broken neck, in his race for the lobby, swinging round stair-posts, taking tight bends like Steve at his peak.

And then he heard the noise, and he almost felt clear and free enough to slow a bit and shout in triumph: for it was the clatter of someone upstairs running urgently into a black kitchen. The yell of a man running crutch-high into a table of stacked pots and trays of cutlery. The agony of someone who couldn't read French, and who couldn't read doors either: for whom the difference between 'Way Out' and 'Kitchen' would have been fine if he'd been reading it in English.

Ronnie hit the street and he didn't stop running until his body hadn't the energy to take him any further. And then sick and faint he crept behind a scraggy bush on a scrub of wasteland and for nearly half an hour he heaved and choked the run out of his system. But he'd made it; he knew that. They'd never find him here. No one would, till he wanted them to. He was too good at this sort of thing for that to happen. Now it was all in the hands of Charlie and the old people: the stupid, great, old dears who, please God, wouldn't turn their backs on the boy....

Then, in the warmth of the morning sun, he slept, and when he woke and he knew for sure it was too late, either way, he set off round the streets till he saw what he was looking for: a gendarme; in a bread shop; one of those coppers with a big gun.

Ronnie kept his eyes off the gun and on the long loaf as the man came out. He sniffed, and scowled, and asked in the low voice Miss Neame knew, ''Ere, mate . . . do you . . . speak . . . English?'

14

Written in the careful, official words on the paper, Ronnie thought his statement sounded like the excuses kids come out at teachers with; and although it was all true his description seemed as unreal as hell in Kingsland's office, in front of Charlie wearing a tie. The only consolation was, there were lots of smiles flashing around, and an air of hope that he'd never felt in anyone's office before. Steve wasn't there, and everyone was a bit vague about exactly how long it would be before he would be free to join them; but Charlie asked about probation, and mentioned a secure job; and Kingsland kept patting his file confidently.

'Anyway, Ronnie, you did all right, son,' the policeman said. 'Spotting that dye, and remembering its significance, that was terrific. . . .'

Ronnie frowned. He didn't quite follow all the words, but obviously the man was well pleased. Well, who wouldn't be?

'So Roy Bradshaw's in custody; and I've heard Bernie's not at home any more; which means a few people round here are going to sleep easier nights. . . .' He smiled, happily. But the real significance of his remark was lost on all but Ronnie and the man he was with. If Bernie was gone, what about Val? Was she still around? Was she back in the flat in Kingston House? Or had she gone with him? That was about it, he thought; that last, that was favourite. She wouldn't show her face round here again. Well, good luck. That was down to her, then. He didn't bloody care, did he? Did he?

Ronnie looked at the other men to see if they could see inside his head. But Kingsland was still going on, all pleased. *He* couldn't, anyway.

'Leave the other Indian business out—the smuggling: let the Immigration boys get over their disappointment. You've done bloody well, Ronnie, because you've used your head, and you've shown some real guts, son. You've done something no one round here's had the courage to do for the last ten years, believe me!' He looked hard at Ronnie; and then he added, 'Revenge, wasn't it? Ronnie's revenge, eh?'

Ronnie frowned before he looked up again. Well, it was and it wasn't. Getting back at them was definitely part of it; but he'd done it to get Charlie off the hook, too, hadn't he? He nodded, anyway.

'Well, you know what they say about revenge?' D.C. Jones put in from the radiator, staring up at the ceiling. 'They call revenge "a kind of wild justice," which the law ought to be weeding out. So where does that leave us, guv?'

'Crap!' said Kingsland. 'You and your fancy words! Listen, Shakespeare, if it wasn't for bloody revenge we'd never nick a tenth of the villains we do. So long as they leave the last bit with us, I'm happy. You know—nothing violent, just mark our card with a bit of plain grassing, or some guts and intelligent thinking, like this lad here....'

They all looked at Ronnie then, who sat up taller in the warmth of the man's genuine praise: not school praise, kid-stakes for doing something the teachers could all do already, but real praise for doing something real, in the real world.

'Yes, I don't mind saying I've got a lot of time for you, son....'

And that seemed to say it all for Ronnie. Somehow it made all the aggravation, the doing without, the running and the hiding worth it all. Whatever happened tomorrow, he thought, he'd got all this in his head to fall back on.

At last it was over, and they drove back to 'The Farm' in Charlie's coach, just the two of them; and Ronnie didn't even notice the long way round they went to avoid Manjit's silent street. He just saw the road ahead, disappearing in patches of oil and smooth new tarmac beneath the wide front of the coach.

After a while, Charlie spoke.

'Elsie and me,' he said, 'we understand, you know....' He kept his eyes unblinking on the traffic. '... About you telling the law ... when you thought we was in with Bradshaw. You 'ad to, we know that....'

Ronnie swallowed, and squirmed in Roy Bradshaw's seat. This was one bit of it they'd gone all round the houses to avoid so far. They'd talked about what had actually happened, about Bradshaw not getting the coach off because of the old people, and about Kingsland waiting for them at Dover. But they hadn't talked about how Kingsland had known, and why Ronnie had done it all on his own. But now Charlie was bringing it all out in the open, trying to make it right....

'Yeah, we understand, Ronnie. I'd have done the same myself, in your position. But I don't know if I'd 'ave 'ad the guts to do what you done for me....'

Ronnie shot an embarrassed look at him. No, he wasn't bumming him up; he meant it—the big man with the wide scarred back.

'And anyway,' Charlie said, his voice low and husky, 'thanks. . . .'

So there it was again! First Kingsland, then Charlie. God, he was going to have to go some to keep this up!

When he got back home he patted the dog and sat down in a comfortable chair in the kitchen with a cup of Elsie's tea.

It was a long time before anyone moved to do anything: and then it was Ronnie.

'Where you going, Ron?'

'Outside....'

'What for?'

'Clean the coach....'

Charlie unfolded his *Sun*. 'Oh, leave it tonight, Ron, for Gawd's sake....'

'No, 'sall right. It's me job, ain't it?' And Ronnie sniffed, and frowned at them, and went out to get on with it.

At school it was as if they'd shifted buildings, so many things were different. Ronnie's desk was out from under the blackboard; some of the kids started to speak to him; and Miss Neame even smiled. All at once, in his own classroom, he didn't feel spare any more. He was somehow part of things. But it was outside it that secretly concerned him most; up in Miss Lessor's group; with that girl. What would happen up there? Because she knew he'd been over to France, in it all. They all did. Was she going to fly at him, spit at him, tear at his face with her nails on account of her old man?

But on the first day back they didn't go to Miss Lessor, and he didn't see her around the school. Perhaps they'd packed up living in London when her old man didn't make it, Ronnie thought. Gone back where they came from, where they belonged. The next day, though, she was there, the same as before, reading all right and trying hard for the teacher. He looked over his word puzzle at her face. It was long and serious, and the eyes had that dull look that comes the morning after crying; that carrying-on, day after the funeral, expression he'd seen on women's faces in the flats: the start of the long job of what people called picking up the threads. He felt lucky. At least when Val had gone he'd had a lot on his mind to get on with.

No, the girl'd leave him alone, he thought.

And Manjit, in her turn, looked at Ronnie. She would never understand him, the strange, spiteful boy whose mother had left him, who was pursued by violent men, and who was mixed up in her family's life in some peculiar way she couldn't understand. He was someone she could never get near to: they lived in different worlds. The strange thing she noticed now, though, in the midst of her unhappiness, was his new, confident air, as if he didn't feel so separate from all the others any more.

And that was one big difference between them. Because the something that had happened had drawn him in; while since that terrible telephone message from France she had been growing very aware that, whatever happened, for people like her in Shepherds Gate there would always be a separateness from those around them.